Lily's Church Camp Adventure

Other Books in the Young Women of Faith Library

The Lily Series
  Here's Lily!
  Lily Robbins, M.D. (Medical Dabbler)
  Lily and the Creep
  Lily's Ultimate Party
  Ask Lily
  Lily the Rebel
  Lights, Action, Lily!
  Lily Rules!
  Rough & Rugged Lily
  Lily Speaks!
  Horse Crazy Lily

Nonfiction
  The Beauty Book
  The Body Book
  The Buddy Book
  The Best Bash Book
  The Blurry Rules Book
  The It's MY Life Book
  The Creativity Book
  The Uniquely Me Book
  The Year 'Round Holiday Book
  The Values & Virtues Book
  The Fun-Finder Book
  The Walk-the-Walk Book
  Dear Diary
  Girlz Want to Know
  NIV Young Women of Faith Bible
  YWOF Journal: Hey! This Is Me
  Take It from Me

Young Women of Faith

Lily's Church Camp Adventure

Nancy Rue

Zonder**kidz**

Zonderkidz.

The children's group of Zondervan

www.zonderkidz.com

Lily's Church Camp Adventure
Copyright © 2003 by Women of Faith

Requests for information should be addressed to:
Zondervan, *Grand Rapids, Michigan 49530*

Library of Congress Cataloging-in-Publication Data

Rue, Nancy N.
    Lily's church camp adventure / Nancy Rue.
       p. cm. — (The Lily Series) (Young women of faith library)
Summary: Learning to sail almost makes up for being separated from the
other Girlz at Camp Galilee in Maine, but twelve-year-old Lily is
homesick, feels like an outsider in her cabin, and makes a choice that
causes Suzy to declare she'll never speak to Lily again.
    ISBN 0-310-70264-X (pbk. : alk. paper)
    [1. Church camps—Fiction. 2. Camps—Fiction. 3. Friendship—Fiction.
4. Christian life—Fiction. 5. Sailing—Fiction. 6. Main—Fiction.]
I. Title. II. Young women of faith
    PZ7.R88515Li 2003
    [Fic]—dc21

                                    2003000550

Published in association with the literary agency of Alive Communications, Inc., 7680 Goddard
Street, Suite 200, Colorado Springs, CO 80920.

Editor: Barbara J. Scott
Interior design: Amy Langeler
Art direction: Michelle Lenger

Printed in the United States of America

03 04 05 06 07 08 09 /❖ DC/ 10 9 8 7 6 5 4 3 2

I still say it's not fair."

Lily Robbins looked up from her suitcase at her younger sister, Tessa, who was letting both arms flop to the bed, over and over and over — and, oh yes, over. Lily knew Tessa would have been doing it with her legs if the body brace she was wearing had let her. It was what she did when she was afraid and wouldn't admit it.

"What are you scared of?" Lily said as she tried to cram one more Camp Galilee T-shirt into her already stuffed duffel bag.

"I'm not scared of nothin'," Tessa said, scowling. "I just said it ain't fair."

"Isn't fair."

"That's what I said!" The arms did a particularly hard flop. "It's not fair that I gotta stay here while you go to some dumb camp for two weeks."

Lily felt her lips twitch. "If it's dumb, why would you want to go anyway?"

Tessa's scowl deepened until Lily was sure her forehead was going to meet her chin. Nobody could scowl like Tessa.

"Besides," Lily said, "you're just now getting back on your feet since the accident. You'd have to sit and watch everybody else hike and rock climb and sail—" She stopped. Tessa's eyes were going into slits.

"Are you scared of being here without me?" Lily said.

"No, that's dumb."

"Are you scared you'll miss me so much you'll cry?"

"That's double dumb!"

Lily climbed on top of her duffel bag and squished it down while she pulled the zipper closed. The bulging sides puckered, and she could almost hear her clothes groaning. She swiveled to face Tessa, who was still trying to maintain the scowl. Lily could see her big green eyes misting up.

"Are you scared I'm not coming back or something?"

"No!" Tessa said. She slammed her arms down so hard that China, Lily's big stuffed panda, bounced two inches off the bed. Tessa turned her glare on him, so that all Lily could see was the wavy back of Tessa's short dark hair. "You're gonna forget about me while you're gone," she said. "That's what's gonna happen."

"No way!" Lily said. She scrambled up and sat next to Tessa on the bed. Otto, Lily's mutt dog, took that as his cue to join them and crawled out from under the bed and hopped up. Lily stroked his head and Tessa's at the same time. "I'm only gonna be gone two weeks," she said. "But even if I was gone the whole summer—or a whole *year* even—I wouldn't forget you. You're my sister."

"Adopted," Tessa muttered. "And I ain't even that yet. That dumb judge still has to make it—what's that word?"

"Official," Lily said. "But I don't need him to do that. You're my sister already, and I'm not gonna forget you, so quit talking like a freak."

Tessa turned to Lily and scoured her face with her eyes as if she were digging for traces of a lie. "Do you *wish* I was goin'?" she said.

"Well, yeah, du-uh!" Lily said. And she did. Tessa was still pretty rowdy and definitely stubborn, but she was nothing like the way she was when she'd first come to live with the Robbins family. Lily was having trouble imagining what it was going to be like not having Tessa tagging after her every minute, asking ten thousand questions. Tessa was what Dad called streetwise, but she didn't know a lot of stuff most nine-year-olds knew. Lily had taken it upon herself to teach her.

If I weren't so jazzed about this camp, Lily thought, *I'd stay home and help Mom and Dad work with her.* But her parents had urged her to go. They said they needed some one-on-one time with Tessa anyway — and Camp Galilee was the best Christian camp for girls in the whole eastern United States — or so everybody said. Mom and Dad were sure that if anybody would enjoy the special programs they had at Galilee, it was Lily.

Besides, the Girlz were all going — Reni and Suzy and Zooey and even Kresha. Their church had made sure Kresha got a scholarship since her mom didn't have a lot of money.

I have to spend all the time I can with my Girlz this summer, Lily thought. *The end of August is gonna be here before I know it, and then I won't see them for a whole year. A whole year!*

"You wanna go real bad," Tessa said. She was still studying Lily's face.

"Yeah, I do," Lily said. She had to be honest with Tessa. The kid had lie radar. "But I also wanna be with you. Too bad I can't be in two places at one time."

Otto gave a growl and wriggled away from Lily, squirming as close to Tessa's side as he could, and sighed himself in. So far, Tessa was the only other person in the Robbins family besides Lily that Otto would even allow to touch him. Ever since she had come home from the hospital, he had to be on the couch or the bed or the chair next to Tessa. The only exception was at night, when, as always, he crawled under Lily's covers like a mole and slept there.

"Look at him," Lily said. "I bet by the time I get back, he'll have forgotten about *me* and only want you."

"Not gonna happen," Tessa said — although the scowl did fade a little at the prospect. "I'll make sure he doesn't forget you." Her eyes suddenly took on an impish gleam. "And I'll make sure Shad Shifferdecker doesn't forget about you either."

Lily felt her blue eyes narrowing. "That's really okay," she said.

"You know he likes you," Tessa said.

Lily grunted and got up to go to the dresser, where she raked a brush through her mane of red curly hair. She could see her usually pale face going blotchy in the mirror.

"You like him too — you know you do," Tessa said.

"Shut *up!*" Lily said.

In the mirror, she could see Tessa grinning.

There was a knock on the door, and Art, Lily's seventeen-year-old brother, poked his head in. "Dad wants to know if your bag is ready yet," he said. "He's got the air conditioner going in the van, and he's ready to roll."

Lily nodded toward her duffel bag and finished the second pigtail she'd just tamed her hair into. She grabbed the khaki hat that matched her shorts and perched it on top of her head. She gazed at her Camp Galilee T-shirt in the mirror. She was a camper from head to toe.

"Good grief — what have you got in here?" Art said. His face went red as he hoisted Lily's bag up onto his shoulder.

"My stuff," Lily said.

"You're going to camp, for Pete's sake," Art said, grunting his way to the door. "All you need's two pairs of shorts and a couple of T-shirts."

"And underwear and socks."

"Nobody changes underwear and socks at camp."

"Gross me out and make me icky!" Lily said. "Just go — oh, wait — I forgot something."

"How could you have forgotten something? Everything you own has to be in this bag."

"Stop! I gotta put my journal in there!"

Lily stuck her hand between her mattresses and pulled out her Talking-to-God Journal and its special purple gel pen.

"Put it in your backpack," Art said as he maneuvered his way out the door. "I'm not picking this thing up again. I'm about to get a hernia as it is."

"What's a hernia?" Tessa said.

"Don't try to come downstairs by yourself, Squirt," Art said to her over his shoulder. "I'll come back and get you for the big tear fest."

"What tear fest?" Lily said, following him down the steps.

"You're leaving for two weeks," Art said. "You're going to cry."

"I am not. Why would I cry?"

"You cry over commercials for AT&T long distance," Art said. "Of course you're gonna cry."

Lily ignored him and jockeyed impatiently from side to side as Art made his way to the first floor and out the front door. Mom was waiting there, and Lily's ten-year-old brother, Joe, was on his knees on a chair behind her, batting at her ponytail like a cat.

"Can I have Lily's share of dessert while she's gone?" he said.

"Sure," Mom said, brown eyes dancing. "And you can also have her share of chores." Her mouth twitched in that way it did instead of outright smiling. Suddenly Lily felt a pang. She wasn't going to see her mom twitch her lips for two whole weeks. She'd never been away from her for longer than a weekend.

"I'm gonna go up and get the Squirt," Art said as he charged through the door and headed for the stairs. Although it was barely light out, his T-shirt was sticking to his back with sweat.

"Too late," Joe said.

Tessa was almost to the bottom of the steps. *One more reason why she can't go to camp,* Lily thought. *She still doesn't do what you tell her to do half the time.*

9

But another shivery pang went through Lily. She was going to miss that too — and Otto — and the horse Big Jake out at the ranch nuzzling her neck with his soft nose. She was even going to miss Joe, the absurd little creep. The wonderful absurd little creep.

"Let's go, Lilliputian," Dad said from the doorway. He was wearing a moustache of perspiration, and even his graying red hair was sparkling with sweat. "I wish I were going to Maine to sit by the bay for two weeks."

And I wish I wasn't! Not without all of you guys!

Lily didn't know where the thought came from, but as Mom hugged her and told her to have an amazing time and not to try to run the place the first day, Lily felt herself fighting back tears. She struggled to keep it from turning into a tear fest only because she didn't want Art to be right. Sniffing while Dad pulled out of the driveway and onto the street, she waved until Tessa was merely a dot on the front porch.

But the minute Kresha bounded out of her apartment building — clothes poking out of her duffel bag, sand-colored hair sticking out of a lopsided ponytail, and a grin spreading ear to ear — Lily's urge to cry disappeared.

"We are going to the camp, Lee-Lee!" Kresha cried. Lily grabbed her hands and jumped up and down with her while Dad shoved Kresha's bag into the van. *I hope no one makes fun of her Croatian accent at camp,* Lily thought before reassuring herself. *Nah — we'll always be there to protect her.*

They both climbed happily into the van, and the happiness built as they picked up each of the Girlz and headed north on the New Jersey Turnpike. They passed around a bag of Doritos to each other — since everyone had been too excited to eat breakfast — and switched seats a half dozen times. And, of course, their mouths ran nonstop.

"Okay — how *cool* is this gonna be, guys?" Reni said.

"You're not scared there won't be any other African-American girls there?" Zooey said. Her brow furrowed under her carefully curled bangs. Zooey was their worrier.

Reni raised an eyebrow at her. "Not that I was even thinking about it," she said, "but my mom checked into it, and there's ten of us."

"Besides," Lily said, "it's not gonna matter because we're all gonna be in the same cabin." She darted her eyes from girl to girl. "You guys did request each other on the form, right?"

"You asked us that eight thousand times," Zooey said.

"And I checked them all when we filled them out," Suzy said, nodding her shiny bob of dark hair.

"Then it's a done deal," Reni said. Suzy, after all, was probably more efficient than the school secretary.

"What we do tonight in our *cabin*?" Kresha said. She'd been practicing saying that word for two weeks.

"Pillow fight," Reni said.

"Unless it's against the rules," Suzy said.

"Let's not tell scary stories," Zooey said. "I won't be able to sleep."

"I say we play a game," Lily said.

Reni grinned slyly. "What kind of game, Lil?"

"I don't know. I'll think of something."

"You do always, Lee-Lee," Kresha said.

Lily nestled back into the seat and smiled to herself. This was going to be the best. She and her Girlz would be together for two weeks with nothing to do but have fun and "discover a relationship with God." That was what the brochure had said. *I'm gonna be good at that,* Lily thought. *I already have one.* She didn't cuddle in with China and Otto and her Talking-to-God Journal every night for nothing.

"You know what I love?" Zooey said.

"What?" Lily said.

"We're not going to have to worry about Chelsea and Ashley and all of them the whole time we're gone."

Reni grunted. "I *don't* worry about them."

But Lily knew what Zooey meant. Chelsea and Ashley and their friends were the popular girls at Cedar Hills Middle School, and they never let the Girlz forget that *they* were never going to be "popular." Even though the Girlz had stopped buying into that and were finding their own happiness, Lily had to agree that it was going to be good not to have to deal with it.

"What about Shad?" Reni said.

Lily snapped her a look. "What about him?" she said.

"Are you glad to be away from him too?" Reni said, dimples going deep into her cheeks.

Lily felt red blotches forming on her neck, like they always did when she wanted to hide her head in a hole. There was a time when she would have answered that question with a loud, "Gross me out and make me icky!" But Shad wasn't so icky anymore, and that was pretty confusing.

"Lily!" Zooey said. "You *do* like him, don't you?"

Only because Lily saw her father's ears practically coming to a point did she not shove an entire Rice Krispies treat into Zooey's mouth. Instead, she said, "Give it up, Zo. I'm not going there."

The scenery changed as the day went on and they wound their way through New England. Trees arched over them, creating a welcome trellis, and Dad told them to roll down their windows so they could smell the air. It was cool on their arms and made Lily want to breathe until her whole chest filled up.

That afternoon they could smell salty air and watch seagulls circling as if they'd been waiting to guide them to Camp Galilee near the ocean. The further they drove, the more clearly Lily could imagine the five of them and their counselor setting out on Penobscot Bay in sailboats with bright striped sails.

"I *really* want to go sailing," she said to the Girlz.

"Doesn't everybody get to sail?" Reni said.

Suzy shook her head. "It says it right in the brochure. Every cabin has a different activity."

"Ours has to be sailing," Lily said. "I've read three books on it."

She didn't add that she hadn't understood most of it. It still sounded like the most exciting thing she could imagine — and she had imagined some pretty exhilarating things in her time.

"I hope we get a counselor that isn't mean," Zooey said.

"Didn't the brochure say all the counselors were college students?" Lily said.

"Yes," Suzy said. "Right on page two."

"Is that what it said?" Dad grinned. "I think I'd better take you home then."

Dad was a college professor. He was always moaning about university students and their shenanigans. Lily didn't care whether they had shenanigans or not — whatever that was. It was going to be cool.

Long after lunch, a sign appeared pointing its arrow down a winding road where they could already see Penobscot Bay. The Girlz all cheered and didn't stop until Dad brought the van to a halt in front of a building that had a big banner on it, which read:

WELCOME TO CAMP GALILEE
REGISTER HERE

"How ya doin'!" said a bubbly, short girl of about nineteen as she opened Lily's door. "Drop your bags over here, and get your cabin assignments over there!"

"What did she say?" Zooey said. She slipped out of the van already chewing on a fingernail. "Put what where?"

"Stick with me, Zo," Reni said.

They all said their good-byes to Dad and took off.

"We'll get all your stuff, Lily," Suzy said. "Don't worry."

Lily wasn't worried, but as Dad held out his arms to hug her, she felt that pang again. He smelled like Dad — like old books and Irish

Spring—and she wouldn't smell that, or get one of his hugs, or sit in his study and talk with him for two whole weeks. At the moment, it might as well have been two years.

"You're going to come home changed, Lilliputian," Dad said into her hair. "I can feel it. This is a sacred place." He held her out by the shoulders to grin at her. "But don't change too much. I want to be able to recognize you when I come to pick you up."

"You are coming back, right?" Lily said.

Surprise flickered through Dad's eyes. "Of course. Two weeks from this very day."

"That's not so long," Lily said.

"It'll go by all too fast."

Lily nodded. She had a huge lump in her throat that was going to explode into tears if Dad didn't get in the van and go and stop smiling at her that way.

"You okay?" he said.

"I'm fine. You can go."

And then she threw her arms around his neck and said, "I love you, Daddy. Write to me."

"I'll do that," he said.

She broke away and ran toward where the Girlz were standing at a long table loaded with folders and staffed by girls who all looked like they could be in Dad's classes.

It's gonna be fine—I'm gonna be with my Girlz, she told herself. *This is gonna be a dream come true and we're gonna have the best cabin in the whole camp.*

The lump disappeared. The pang faded. She was smiling by the time she got to her little cluster of Girlz.

"What cabin are we in?" she said.

They all turned to her. Zooey was wild-eyed, and the others weren't much calmer.

"What's wrong?" Lily said.

14

"Me and Suzy are in the same cabin," Zooey said, eyes swimming. "But we're not with you guys."

"Kresha and I are together," Reni said. She bit her lip. "But, Lil, you're not with any of us. You're in a whole other cabin."

"Nuh-uh," Lily said.

The pang came back. Only this time, it was a full-fledged pain.

Chapter 2

Lily just stared at the paper Reni handed her. There it was in black and white:

Asher Cabin
Robbins, Lily

The rest of the names disappeared in a blur of tears, but it didn't matter. None of them belonged to her Girlz.

"This has to be a mistake," she said through the lump in her throat. "We all said we wanted to be in the same cabin."

"I asked about that," Reni said. "They said we would have taken up one whole cabin, and they knew we'd hang out together all the time and never meet anybody else."

I don't want to meet anybody else! Lily wanted to cry.

But the faces that looked back at her were all as stricken as she knew hers was. Whatever she did, they would do, and then some. Nobody could sob like Zooey. Nobody could retreat into herself like a snail the way Suzy did. Nobody could pitch fits like Kresha or argue like Reni.

Lily sucked in a deep breath. "It's just where we sleep," she said. "We can do everything else together."

"Do you promise?" Zooey said.

"Yes," Reni said. "We'll get to hang together — don't freak or anything."

"Come, Reni," Kresha said. "We go."

"We're in Zebulun Cabin," Reni called back over her shoulder as Kresha dragged her away.

"Why can't they give these cabins names you can pronounce?" Zooey said, still furrowing her forehead over the cabin list. "Naph … what?"

"Naphtali," Suzy said. She looked at Lily with sad eyes. "Are you gonna be all right, Lily?"

"Sure," Lily said. "We'll all sit together at dinner."

That seemed to reassure Suzy, but it didn't do much for Lily as she dragged her duffel bag and backpack down a sandy path that threaded its way into a stand of trees. Snuggled among them was a white, square clapboard building with a green roof and windows that wrapped all the way around and were covered with screens. Green rolls of canvas hung over each one, lifting and sighing back down in the breeze. It would have started daydreams in Lily's head if that same head hadn't been so full of the real world.

But she sucked in some air again and made her way up the little wooden steps. The screen door opened, and a woman of about forty smiled down at her. All Lily could think was, *She's wearing dentures. I think she's wearing dentures.*

"You have to be Lily," the woman said. "You look just like your picture — I would have known you anywhere."

She put out her hand, and Lily fumbled to get both of her bags onto one arm so she could shake hands. The woman grinned and grabbed the duffel bag.

"Oh, sorry," Lily said, and felt stupid. She followed the lady into the cabin.

"You certainly came prepared," the woman said as she set Lily's bag down with a grunt. She wiped her hands on the back of her denim shorts and put out her hand. "Now let's shake. I'm Jackie. I'll be your counselor."

"Oh," Lily said.

So much for all the counselors being college students. This lady was older than Lily's mom. She had some gray hairs among the rest, which were kind of a faded peanut color, and wrinkles around her brown eyes that crinkled up like spider webs when she smiled. *She couldn't look less like a college student if she tried,* Lily thought. She was wearing battered hiking shoes and a shirt like Lily's dad wore when he played golf.

"You're not the first to arrive," Jackie was saying. "Meet two of your cabin mates."

She swept a tanned arm toward two girls Lily hadn't noticed before. They were unpacking suitcases side by side, and when they looked up at Lily, her heart sank.

They were both beautiful—as beautiful as Ashley and Chelsea. No, even prettier. One had thick, straight, light brown hair streaked with blonde, soft brown eyes, and a tan that made her look as if she'd spent the winter in Hawaii. The other one looked like pictures of fairies Lily had seen in storybooks, with short, blonde, wispy hair and little, twinkly blue eyes. Both of them were dressed as if they had bought out The Gap.

"This is Alexandria," Jackie said, nodding to the girl with the Rapunzel-long hair, "and this is Genevieve."

Lily suddenly wished she had a beautiful name—and that she wasn't wearing a Camp Galilee T-shirt and baggy khaki shorts—and that she was safely tucked into a cabin with her Girlz.

"This is Lily," Jackie said.

The two girls half-smiled and murmured hellos. Lily gave a weak "hi" and looked at Jackie.

"Where do I put my stuff?" she said.

"Alexandria and Genevieve have claimed the two beds on that end," she said, pointing. "Any of the other three is fair game."

Lily scurried to one at the other end, one bed from the wall.

"There are drawers for your things under the bed," Jackie said. "Whatever you can't stuff in there can stay in your bag, and we'll put it in the closet." Lily looked around in time to see Jackie grin. "And from what I can tell, you're all going to have a surplus. Holler if you need anything."

When she turned to go into what must have been her private little nook, Lily was reminded of Mom — her outdoorsy look, her deep voice, her dry sense of humor. The pain in her chest went deeper.

"So where do you live?" Alexandria said.

"Who, me?" Lily said.

Genevieve gave a little giggle. "She already knows where I live. I'm her next-door neighbor."

Wonderful, Lily thought as her heart sank further. *They already know each other. They're probably best friends. So much for me.*

"I'm from Jersey," she mumbled.

"Oh," they both said.

There was a stiff silence. Both girls looked down at their suitcases, and then Genevieve suddenly popped her head up and said, "Have you ever been to this camp before?"

"No," Lily said. She was afraid to say too much for fear that the eye rolling and hair tossing would begin. That was the way it usually was with pretty, popular, well-dressed girls. Better not to give them too much information to use against her later. Then again, if she didn't say anything at all they'd probably start calling her a mute or something.

"No," she said again. "I've never been here before."

"I have!"

That came from the doorway, where a dark-haired, dark-skinned girl was bursting her way in, backpacks askew and cheeks bright red, as if the energy she had inside was sizzling right through her skin.

19

"I'm D. J.," she said, tossing all three backpacks onto the nearest bed. "Who are you guys?"

There was a stunned silence, and then Genevieve giggled for no apparent reason.

"She's Alexandria," she said, nudging her friend.

"She's Genevieve,' Alexandria said, nudging back.

D. J. looked at Lily, who had no one to identify her.

"I'm Lily," she said.

"Cool!" D. J. said. "Isn't this place just the best?"

She jumped up on the bed on all fours — reminding Lily painfully of Otto — and crawled over to put her face against the screen. She took a deep breath and sat back on her knees, grinning. "It still smells the same."

"Were you in this cabin last year?" Genevieve said.

"Nuh-uh. I wasn't in any cabin. My parents were the cooks, so I got to spend the whole summer here — only I wasn't a camper. It's not as fun if you aren't a camper — but now I am, and I am so jazzed."

Ya think? Lily wanted to say. She was sure D. J. was going to start jumping up and down on the mattress any minute. And she was sure it would be adorable if she did. D. J. wasn't drop-dead gorgeous like the other two, but with her bright, sparkly brown eyes, olive skin, and cute husky voice, she was probably one of the popular kids at her school. She would be here too, Lily was sure of that. The way she was chattering away and lounging against the pillows, she looked as if she were completely at home. Lily was feeling taller and ganglier and more redheaded by the second.

"So do you know what kind of stuff we're gonna be doing?" Genevieve said.

"Yes — and it's all awesome," D. J. said. She sat up cross-legged, her face animated as if she were about to tell a story. Alexandria and Genevieve stopped pulling The Gap out of their suitcases and drew closer. Lily kept unpacking, but she listened.

"We do Bible study — which isn't boring at all — and then activities — and then lunch — the food here is great — well, at least it was last year because my parents were cooking it — but anyway, then we have a rest period, and then in the afternoon your cabin does its assigned thing — like some cabins do hiking and some do rock climbing — "

"They do it by cabin?" Lily said.

"Oh, yeah. The cabin does everything together the first week so you'll bond, and then — "

"Define 'everything,'" Lily said.

D. J. cocked her head of short, shiny dark hair at Lily. "Like — everything. We eat together, do Bible study and activities together. You can do anything you want at free time, but most girls hang with their cabin mates." D. J.'s eyes got even shinier. "Then the second week you get your cabin project. That week you can eat with other cabins and stuff, but you're so busy working on your project you just sort of end up staying together. You're supposed to be building a community — I think that's what they called it. Anyway — you get totally close to the girls in your cabin. It's awesome!"

She looked at the three of them as if she already felt close to them. Lily felt as far away as if she were still at home.

I don't get to eat with the Girlz? she thought. *I can't sit by them at Bible study? I'm gonna be a jerk if I don't hang with my cabin during free time?*

Her heart took its final dive, right to the pit of her stomach.

"Okay, you guys," D. J. was saying. "I know our other girl isn't here yet, but when she gets here, we have to make a pact to be, like, *the* best cabin in the whole camp. Asher is going to *rule!*"

"Uh-huh," Lily said.

Suddenly two weeks seemed like an eternity.

By the time she and the other girls in the cabin finished unpacking, it was suppertime. Jackie walked with them back up the sandy path to the main walkway, which led up another hill to the dining hall.

D. J. chattered all the way, with Jackie and Genevieve asking the questions. Alexandria remained quiet, like Lily, only she didn't look nearly as awkward about it as Lily felt.

"You know what's really cool about this camp being named Galilee?" D. J. said.

"No," Jackie said. "But I bet we're about to find out."

"The Galilee in the Bible once belonged to Assyria. I'm Syrian!"

"Is that why your skin is so dark?" Genevieve said. "I mean, no offense."

"No — it's cool. I'm proud of my heritage," D. J. said.

Lily saw her chance to contribute to the conversation. "My best friend is African-American," she said, "and she's proud of that too."

But a massive clanging sound drowned out every word. They all put their hands over their ears.

"What's that?" Genevieve shouted.

"Dinner's ready!" D. J. shouted back.

There was a crowd under the sign on the dining hall that read:

LET US BREAK BREAD TOGETHER

As soon as the bell stopped, the double screen doors opened and the crowd of girls jostled its way in. Lily stood on her tiptoes, straining to see Reni or Zooey or Kresha or Suzy, but the campers all blended together.

It wasn't until Asher cabin was settled at its assigned table that Lily spotted any of them. While the camp director — a woman tall as a statue with bright white hair — prayed over the food, Lily peeked around and was able to locate Suzy at the Naphtali table. When the blessing was over and Lily could really look, she saw Zooey beside her. As the food was passed, they both shook their heads at it and stared miserably down at their plates.

Lily found herself breathing a sigh of relief. Seeing that they were obviously as unhappy as she was made her feel a little closer to them.

She waved in their direction — nearly knocking a huge bowl of salad right out of D. J.'s hands — but neither one of them would look up. Lily let her eyes roam until she found the Zebulun table.

There was Kresha, in the center on one side, talking away, hands flying, and eyes darting all around. The other girls at the table were all leaning toward her, taking in every word — including Reni.

Reni's eyes were rounded and her dimples were in full view. Lily knew that meant she was glued to what was going on around her. And she was liking it.

"Reni!" Lily hissed.

It was ridiculous, of course. There was so much high-pitched talking going on in the hall, she would have had to stand up on the bench and yell to get Reni's attention. And even then, Reni probably couldn't have been torn away.

"Do you want some spaghetti, Lindy?" D. J. said at her elbow.

"It's Lily," Lily said in a wooden voice. "And no, thanks. I don't feel like eating right now."

Chapter 3

After supper—where everything tasted like chewed-up cardboard in Lily's mouth—the whole camp convened in a large, carpeted room with whitewashed wood walls and an arched window that looked out over the bay. Some girls were oohing and aahing over the view, but Lily just gave it a glance, took in a sailboat and a couple of seagulls, and then searched the room for the Girlz.

"Asher cabin is sitting right over here," Jackie said near Lily's ear. She touched her elbow in a way that added, *You'll be expected to sit with us.*

Feeling as if she had just been scolded, Lily ducked her head and dutifully followed Jackie to the spot where Alexandria and Genevieve were huddled together on the floor. D. J. was standing up next to them, bouncing up to swat at one of the oversized beach balls the counselors were chucking out into the crowd. D. J. missed, and the ball smacked Lily right in the forehead.

It didn't really hurt, but tears burned in Lily's eyes as she sank down next to the Alexandria-Genevieve unit.

I've been bombarded with enough stuff today, she thought. *I don't need beach balls in the face too.*

The tall, white-haired lady suddenly appeared at the front, and every ball and foam-rubber slingshot obediently made its way to the floor.

"Good evening, girls," she said into a microphone. "I am Mary Francis McCall—and for the next two weeks, I'm going to be your mom."

A cheer went up the likes of which only fifty middle-school girls could make. Lily joined in only half-heartedly.

She's not my mom, she thought. *Not even close. I wish my mom was here.* Tears started to well up again. Mary Francis was going on about all the things D. J. had already told them in the cabin, so Lily searched the room once again for her Girlz. She spotted Suzy and Zooey in the very next group. They were clinging to each other just the way Alexandria and Genevieve were.

At least they've got each other, Lily thought. She had Jackie and the other three girls in Asher within six inches, but she felt as if she were all by herself. All the girls, the counselors, and Mary Francis seemed to be floating around in another world that she was sitting outside of looking in.

"What we're all about for the next two weeks, girls," Mary Francis was saying, "is building God-relationships. Our prayer is that you'll grow closer to each other and closer to God."

The girls all cheered as if they'd just been told there would be hot fudge sundaes for everyone. Lily decided they would have cheered over just about anything. She didn't cheer for this one.

I already have God-relationships, she thought. *I came here to be with those people.*

"Normally we will have a program for you at this time," Mary Francis said. "But tonight you're tired from getting here, and we want you to have some time to get settled in and get acquainted with your cabin mates." She smiled at the group. "Early to bed, ladies."

They even cheered over that, and Lily joined in. Not only did she feel wiped out — all she wanted to do was bury her face in her pillow and cry.

Maybe if I just get it all out, she thought, *I won't have to be holding back tears every second.*

"All right, girls, stay close," Jackie said as they all stood up to go. "That little cabin can be hard to find in the dark."

"I can lead!" D. J. said.

And she did, with the rest of them following her at a dead run. Twice Lily almost tripped over Alexandria-Genevieve, and as it was, she missed a step into the cabin and fell headlong through the door — right into somebody's arms.

"It's about time you all showed up," that somebody said.

"Are you Maggie?" Jackie said.

"Oh — our last cabin mate!" D. J. said. She jumped over a bed to get to Maggie to shake her hand. "I'm D. J.," she said. "How ya doin'?"

"What does D. J. stand for?" Maggie said.

Genevieve giggled. Lily was getting used to her laughing for what appeared to be no reason. What did surprise her was the way Maggie was curiously studying D. J. through her little wire-rimmed glasses. She was more in-your-face than Tessa.

But as far as Lily could tell, Maggie was unlike Tessa in every other way. She was almost as tall as Lily and reminded her of a bird. Her smallish dark eyes darted restlessly, and her almost-curly brown hair was pulled back into a feathery ponytail, which twitched constantly as she tilted and cocked and slanted her head in every direction.

"What's everybody else's name?" she said. She turned to Alexandria. "Start with you."

"She's Alexandria," Genevieve said.

"She's Genevieve," Alexandria said.

"Do you always talk for each other?" Maggie said.

"Alexandria doesn't talk for me." Genevieve looked at her friend. "Do you?"

"And what about you? Don't you talk?"

Lily realized with a start that Maggie was speaking to her.

"Yeah, I talk," Lily said. It occurred to her that no one had ever asked her *that* question before.

"So what's your name?" Maggie said.

"Lily."

"Oh. You mean like the flower?"

"Kind of, yeah."

Jackie cleared her throat. "I'm Jackie. I'm your counselor."

Maggie gaped at her openly. "*You* are the counselor?"

Jackie grinned. "I'm obviously not one of the campers."

"I thought all the counselors were college students."

"I am a college student," Jackie said.

"You *are*?" D. J. said. "That's so cool!"

"But aren't you like the oldest one ever?" Maggie said.

"Sometimes it feels that way," Jackie said. "All right, girls, lights out in fifteen minutes. A couple of you need to shower tonight, or you'll run out of hot water in the morning."

"I can't take a shower at night," Maggie said. "I'll get a chill and then a cold and then it'll turn into pneumonia."

"I'll go tonight," Lily said. A private shower might be a good place to cry.

She tried to be quiet about it, which really wasn't necessary because D. J. was in the shower next to her, singing at the top of her lungs. Somebody from the next cabin down the path yelled for her to keep it down. It didn't seem to bother D. J.

I wish I felt as at home here as she does, Lily thought.

When she finally slipped into her pajamas and out of the bathroom, the lights were out and everyone was in bed. Maggie had taken the last bed, against the wall next to Lily. Mary Francis obviously didn't know Maggie, because she didn't look the least bit tired from traveling. She was propped up on one elbow, as if she'd been waiting impatiently for Lily to get there so she could grill her.

"So where do you live?" she said in a low voice. Jackie must have given the order to talk in whispers.

"I'm from Jersey," Lily said. That was usually a conversation stopper.

"What part?" Maggie said.

"Burlington. It's in — "

"That's in South Jersey. How many brothers and sisters you got?"

"Two brothers. Oh — and a sister."

Maggie's bird head came to attention. "What's wrong with the sister?"

"Nothing!"

"It was like you almost forgot about her."

"We just adopted her," Lily said.

"Is she a baby?"

"No — she's nine."

"Didn't her parents want her?"

"My parents are her parents now."

Lily glanced over at D. J.'s bed. Maybe she could pull her into this interrogation so she didn't have to feel like Maggie was going to read her her rights any second. But D. J. was already snoozing.

"You have any hobbies?" Maggie said.

Lily looked back at her. Did the girl have a set of index cards with questions written on them? There was no way she could be thinking of things to ask this fast without notes.

"Do you?" Lily said.

"I asked you."

"I have a couple of different hobbies. My friends and I — "

"Who's your best friend? Do you have one?"

"Yes, I have one! She's here in camp, actually, in Zebulun Cabin. All my best friends are here — all four of them. We wanted to all be in the same cabin, but they wouldn't let us. I didn't think it would be so bad, but the way they have things set up here, I'm not even going to get to see them or anything."

Lily had to stop to take a breath. Maggie had tilted her head in three directions during that paragraph.

"Oh," she said. "That must be why you don't talk that much."

"I talk!" Lily said.

"Not that much. I guess that's because you already have all the friends you need."

Lily felt a little stung, and she peered at Maggie through the dark. Maggie was just looking at her, ponytail twitching.

"When I was all talking about the Girlz," Lily said, "I didn't mean, like — you know — that I don't want to talk to anybody else."

"Yeah, but maybe you don't," Maggie said. "Well, good night."

And then she cheerfully rolled over and within seconds was taking deep, even breaths.

I do want to talk! Lily wanted to cry out to her. *But not right now. Right now I want to talk to Reni and Kresha and make sure they still want to be with me. I wanna see if Suzy and Zooey are okay — and Tessa. I want to say goodnight to Mom and Dad and Joe and Art and Otto and China. I want Otto right here in the bed with me.*

That did it. She planted her face in her pillow and cried herself to sleep.

When she woke the next morning, it was to the screaming and whining of what sounded like an entire flock of seagulls right in her bedroom. Only when she opened her eyes and felt them burn from crying did she remember she was at camp. She groped around for her pillow to put it over her head and saw D. J. sitting up, face pressed to the screen.

"Listen to those seagulls," she whispered. "Isn't that awesome?"

29

"Uh-huh," Lily said.

"They're actually just called gulls, not seagulls," Maggie said.

"How'd you know that?" D. J. said. She situated herself on the bed so she could see Maggie. D. J.'s brown eyes were barely open, but they were as bright as they'd been the day before.

Yikes, she loves everything, Lily thought.

"I had to learn all the species of birds," Maggie said. "If I hear a black-billed magpie, I definitely remember that one because people like to call me Mag-Pie instead of Maggie." She gave D. J. and Lily a narrow-eyed look. "And don't even think about it."

Lily didn't. All she could think about was the Girlz. If she was this miserable, she couldn't imagine how Suzy and Zooey must feel.

I have to pull myself together for them, she decided.

Lily found them both in the breakfast line, and without looking back at the ever-watchful Jackie, she made a beeline for them. Just as she'd expected, Suzy was looking around as if she'd been hit over the head with something and didn't quite know where she was. When she saw Lily, she lunged for her, arms wide.

"Are you okay?" Lily said as she hugged her.

"No!" Suzy said. "I miss you — and Reni — and Kresha!"

"Me too," Lily said. "I'm hating being apart from you guys." She pulled back from Suzy a step. "How's Zooey doing?"

"Hey, Lily!"

Lily looked up to see Zooey standing right next to her, face a wreath of smiles. Beside her was a red-cheeked girl who was grinning equally as widely. They looked like a pair of Cheshire cats.

"This is Emmy!" Zooey said. "She's in the cabin with Suzy and me." Zooey gave Emmy's shoulders a squeeze. "Emmy was feeling homesick last night, so me and Suzy told her she could be with us."

"Oh," Lily said. Nothing else would come out of her mouth. It was as if everything were stuck in her throat.

The bell rang just then, and Jackie called out to Lily.

"I'll see you — sometime," Lily said to Suzy.

"You promised we could eat together," Suzy said. Her eyes were filling up.

"For Pete's sake, Suzy," Zooey said. "She doesn't run the camp. That's the rule."

"Yo, Lily," Jackie said.

Lily gave Suzy one last hug and hurried back to the Asher group. Maggie was staring at her. She didn't stop staring until they were sitting at the table across from each other.

"What?" Lily said to her.

"I was right, wasn't I?" Maggie said.

"About what?"

"About what we talked about last night," Maggie said. "I was right."

Lily didn't answer as she stabbed a pancake onto her plate with her fork.

"Yep," Maggie said. "You think you've got all the friends you need already."

Chapter

4

Bible study was the first thing on the agenda after breakfast. Asher cabin had a corner of the big room where they'd met the night before. There were big, squishy pillows for them to sit on this time, and Lily sank gratefully into one. She was already tired.

"I thought this was supposed to be Bible study," Maggie said. She was going from pillow to pillow, poking each one with her fingers as if to make sure she got the softest one.

"It is Bible study," D. J. said.

"Then where are the Bibles?"

Lily looked around. Alexandria and Genevieve were shrugging.

"So God created man — and woman — in his own image," Jackie said as she sailed into the corner with a roll of white paper and a stack of magazines. "'In the image of God he created him; male and female he created them.'" She plopped the stuff down in the center of their circle of pillows and produced five pairs of scissors from one of the many pockets on her khaki vest. "That's your Bible verse for the day."

"I know it's from Genesis," Genevieve said. "Chapter one."

"It's like verse twenty-seven or something," Lily said.

"That's exactly what it is," Jackie said. "Good job, Lily."

The rest of them blinked at her for a minute.

Wonderful, Lily thought. *I finally open my mouth and now they probably all think I'm a know-it-all.*

She was surprised that Maggie hadn't beaten her to it. *She seems to know everything else in the world. Probably because she asks so many questions,* Lily thought. *No wonder they called her Mag-Pie.* She hoped she didn't slip and call her that herself.

"So what *is* your image?" Jackie was saying as she handed out the scissors. "If you know who you really are, really and truly, deep down inside, that will bring you closer to God — because God is the one who created you that way. Make sense?"

She looked at Maggie as if she were expecting an argument, but Maggie was too busy eyeing the magazines.

"I'd like for you to search for images of yourself in these magazines," Jackie went on. "Not pictures of the fashion models you *want* to be — and I don't doubt some of you will be — but things that truly represent the real you. Maybe it will just be colors or shapes or words."

Now this is cool, Lily thought. *This is way cool!*

She could barely wait for Jackie to stop giving the instructions so she could dig in. The other girls began to chat and giggle as they thumbed through *Brio* and *Travel & Leisure,* but Lily lost herself in the world of pictures. If there was anything she could do, it was make a collage — or a scrapbook, a photo album, a journal. And if there was anything she knew about, it was who she was.

She was already pasting her pictures into place before the other girls had all of theirs cut out.

"How'd you do that so fast?" Maggie said.

"Because she didn't stop and read every article," D. J. said, nudging Maggie with her elbow as if they were old pals.

"It's one of my hobbies," Lily said.

"You mean you sit around and make these all the time?" Maggie said.

"Not exactly — " Lily started to say.

But she stopped and watched Maggie's eyes suddenly catch on something in the *Time* magazine she was holding. They immediately began to dart back and forth across an article on anthrax.

"She's gone," D. J. said.

Maggie had only half a collage done when Jackie called time.

"All right, girls," Jackie said. "Let's go around the circle and have each one of you tell us about your image, as you've shown it on your collage."

Genevieve giggled — of course — and Alexandria scooted back so she had one shoulder behind her. Maggie tilted her little bird head toward her collage as if it had just dawned on her that it was supposed to mean anything.

D. J. will go first and get everybody started, Lily thought. *Then maybe we'll run out of time, and I won't have to do it.*

It didn't matter at that moment that she had once won a speech contest — or that she loved to be on stage doing Shakespeare — or that this past school year she had been class president and spoken in front of the entire seventh grade. At that moment, all she knew was that if she opened her mouth to speak to her cabin mates, it was going to come out all wrong. *After all,* she thought, *everything I've said so far has.*

But Jackie looked right at her and said, "Lily, why don't you share first?"

"Go, Lily," D. J. said. It occurred to Lily right then that D. J. was probably a cheerleader at her school. A girl's popularity doubled the minute she took pom-poms in hand.

"So what's that big bright light thing in the middle?" Maggie said as she leaned across D. J. to get a closer view of Lily's collage.

"Let's let Lily just tell about it," Jackie said.

Maggie tapped the collage. "So go already," she said.

34

"Um, well," Lily began eloquently, "my image is that I'm a lot of different things and they all come from gifts God has given me — that's the big sun in the middle. Like I try to be beautiful — well, not beautiful, but you know, the best I can look — I learned that when I did modeling." She pointed to the girl going down a runway, coming out of the sun. She hurried on before anyone could snicker. "And I try to take care of my body because it's been given to me by God to take care of, and that's all like nutritious food and stuff on here that I learned about in this class I took. And I try to be a good friend because my friends are way important to me." She stopped and swallowed hard. Now would not be a good time to cry. *Why,* she wondered, *can I still cry after all the tears I poured out last night?* She pointed to the confetti she had made and sprinkled over the collage. "This is for the parties I like to give — I like to make everything all cool for people — and this bunch of words is for when I wrote for the school newspaper — I had this advice column — because I like to write and stuff — and I also like to act — I was in two Shakespeare Festivals so that's what this is about."

She made a lame stab with her finger at the mask she'd put together from several colors and bit her lip. *They think I'm such a bragger by now,* she thought. *I'm done talking.*

Maggie continued to inspect the collage. "So you're into politics and horses and camping too," she said, as if Lily had invited her to finish up for her.

"Yeah," Lily said. "That's about it."

"What do you mean that's about it?" D. J. said. "You do a lot of stuff!"

"Wow," Genevieve said.

Jackie nodded at her. "What wow? Tell Lily."

"Well, no offense," Genevieve said, "but I thought you were way too shy to do all this stuff."

"I'm not shy," Lily said. "Really — I'm not."

"I bet you're like this leader in your school," D. J. said.

Lily thought she saw a sheen of admiration in D. J.'s eyes. It melted the lump in her chest just a little.

Maybe they're starting to like me, Lily thought. *Now that they know I'm not some freak.*

It was a hopeful thought, and it was a better one than the nagging notion that all the other Girlz except Suzy were getting along fine. She clung to it.

Until it was time to move on to the big group activity outside. Then Alexandria and Genevieve attached at the hip again, and D. J. walked beside Maggie, answering her never-ending questions. Lily walked alone behind them.

It wasn't more than a few seconds before Jackie caught up with her and slung her arm around her shoulders, but it didn't help.

She has to do this, Lily thought. *It's her job.*

The pain was back in full force when lunch was over and the girls settled into the cabin for an hour of quiet time. Alexandria and Genevieve passed notes to each other, D. J. sat with her nose against the screen smelling the sea air, and Maggie stuck her face in a book entitled *Gray's Anatomy.* The loneliness descended on Lily, and she pulled out a piece of paper and a gel pen and wrote:

Dear Mom and Dad,
  Here I am at Camp Galilee.

She stopped and sighed. *Duh! They know I'm at Camp Galilee!* If she hadn't written it in ink, she would have erased it.

There are five girls in my cabin: Asher. There's D. J. — only I don't know what that stands for — and Maggie, and Alexandria and Genevieve. Those last two already knew each other from home. Our counselor is Jackie. She's not a college student. Well, she is — but she's like an adult. Older than Mom. Not that that's old. I think she wears false teeth.

We get up at 7:30 a.m. and have breakfast at 8:00 a.m. Everyone in our cabin sits together at every meal. After cabin clean-up, we have Bible study and then outside activities and then lunch. Now we're having quiet time, and in the afternoon, we do our cabin's sport. I don't know what ours is yet, but I hope it's sailing. Then we have free time where we can do crafts or swim or other stuff I don't know about yet. We have supper and then evening program. It's busy.

Lily stopped again. Usually she could write and write and write until her hand cramped up. She was used to not even putting down her pen — especially since Otto liked to chew gel pens and would snatch one right out of her fingers if she even loosened her grip on it.

Her eyes got teary again as she thought about Otto. That was what she really wanted to write about — how much she missed everybody, even the Girlz.

She put the tip of her pen to the paper, but she didn't write.

How can I tell Mom and Dad I practically hate it here, she thought, *when they paid all that money for me to come, and Dad drove all the way up here to bring us, and they have enough to worry about with Tessa?*

She couldn't tell them, of course. Instead she asked them to say hi to Joe and Art and Tessa and Otto and China and Big Jake if they saw him. Then she signed her name, folded the letter, and sealed it into an envelope.

Lily expected to feel better after she talked to them on paper. But she didn't feel as if that had been her talking at all.

Jackie poked her head in from her little nook. For a crazy instant, Lily wondered if she had mail for them. Dad had promised to write every day.

It's only been twenty-four hours, she told herself. *It seems like about a year.*

"Girls, you have fifteen more minutes," Jackie said. "I want to encourage you to spend that time just having a talk with God about what you learned about yourself and each other this morning."

Lily waited for Genevieve to giggle, which she did. Lily realized then that she hadn't seen either Alexandria or Genevieve roll her eyes yet. It surprised her, but she didn't let her guard down. Both of them had made beautiful collages full of flowers and birds and pretty faces. Maybe they weren't the in-crowd type like Ashley and Chelsea, but if they got any more perfect, Lily was sure she was going to throw up.

"Spend quiet time with God," Maggie whispered to Lily when Jackie left the room. "Does she mean pray?"

"Yeah," Lily whispered back.

"Like recite the Lord's Prayer?"

"Maybe. Or just talk to God."

"Like I know how to do that," Maggie said.

"Quiet time with God, not each other," Jackie said from the nook.

Maggie closed her eyes. Lily thought for the first time of her Talking-to-God Journal, which was tucked into one of the drawers under the bed.

I didn't even think about that last night! she thought. *That's because I was so tired — and because I didn't have China and Otto to do it with me.*

She could do it now — but Lily didn't reach down and open the drawer. There were too many what-ifs.

What if Genevieve and Alexandria did their first eye rolling because Lily was writing to God? What if it seemed silly to them? What if perfect people didn't have to write out their prayers?

What if D. J. told her they didn't do that at Camp Galilee? That it all had to be actual prayers?

What if Maggie asked her a bazillion questions about it — or worse, grabbed it out of her hand to read it?

Lily shook her head and closed her eyes. Maybe she could just play it safe and journal in her mind.

Her thoughts were a jumble — not even close to being organized the way they were when she wrote them down. They were like the pieces of confetti on her collage, only they wouldn't stay in one place. They kept bouncing around as if they were continually being knocked loose.

I don't want to be left out in the cabin — but I want to be with my Girlz, not these people who don't know anything about me — but now I don't even want to be here at all because I miss Mom and Dad and everybody so much — and even if I go home, I don't think I even know how to be me anymore. I've only been gone one day — and I feel like some whole other person.

"You're going to come home changed," Dad had said.

But not this way! Lily thought. She was fighting back tears again.

Please, God — at least let me be Lily again!

"Amen," Jackie said.

Lily jumped. Jackie was standing in the middle of the cabin wearing sunglasses and a layer of something white and thick on her nose.

"Anybody want to go sailing?" she said.

Chapter 5

"Are you serious?" D. J. said. She was actually standing up on her bed.

"Serious as a heart attack," Jackie said.

"Huh?" Maggie said.

But the cheer that went up in the cabin drowned her out. Even Lily joined in.

"Put on your bathing suits under your shorts," Jackie said. "Be ready with sunscreen and a towel and a hat in seven minutes. If you tend to burn, bring along a light shirt too." She looked at Lily. "That means you, girlfriend."

"And Genevieve," Alexandria said. "She fries in the sun."

"Alexandria doesn't," Genevieve said. "She tans like no other."

"Not a problem for me, either," D. J. said. She was yanking everything out of her drawers and tossing it over her shoulder.

"Yeah, but that's your ethnicity," Maggie said.

D. J. stopped rooting for her swimsuit and puckered her brow at Maggie. "I don't think I have that."

"You're Syrian," Maggie said. Then she looked at Lily. "You're probably Irish."

"English," Lily said. She already had her sunscreen and her shirt wrapped in a towel, and she was waiting impatiently for Alexandria and Genevieve to come out of the potty stalls so she could slip into her swimsuit.

"You know what I bet?" Maggie said. "I bet if all your freckles grew together, you'd have a great tan."

Lily looked up to see Maggie studying her back, which she knew had about a hundred freckles per square inch. Joe had been reminding her of that ever since he could talk.

But Maggie's comment couldn't dampen the excitement Lily was feeling — for the first time in a whole day.

Sailing. She'd dreamed about it ever since she'd seen the pictures in the Camp Galilee brochure — girls manning the billowing striped sails of a sailboat, their hair blowing as they laughed into the wind. The words from the library book she'd read flooded back to her now — *a small sloop ghosting out of a harbor soon after sunrise. At dusk the sloop returns. The faces of the sailors are flushed from the sun.*

It was *the* most awesome thing she could think of — and now she was going to get to do it.

"How cool is this?" D. J. said to her as they charged toward the bathroom.

"Way cool," Lily said.

As they followed Jackie down the path to the bay, Lily hung back a little while the other girls chattered. She *wanted* to be alone this time, just to concentrate on the things she'd learned from the book — and from watching ten minutes of a special on the Discovery Channel before Art had taken over the remote.

Port was one side of the boat and starboard was the other — only at the moment she couldn't remember which was which. She was pretty sure the bow was the front and the stern was the back. Then there was, like, tack and jibe — which kind of sounded like the name of a rock band—and windward and lee. That could have been the name of a law firm.

But it didn't matter that it was all bouncing merrily around in her head and making no sense. She was about to learn it *all* for real.

I know I can do anything if I put myself into it one hundred percent, she thought. *Especially if it's something I think I'm supposed to be doing—like it's part of me.*

"Have you ever sailed before?" Maggie said at her elbow.

"No," Lily said, "but I know some stuff about it."

"I've been on a sailboat," Maggie said. "We went on a cruise to the Bahamas from New York and back last fall. That was a fifty-eight-foot boat though, and nobody would let me do anything."

"Wow," Lily said. "That would still be way cool."

"Not when it's a floating home-school classroom." Maggie pinched in her face and spoke in a nasal voice. "'Just enjoy the ride and get your work done, Margaret.'"

"Oh," Lily said. Personally, she thought it would be close to heaven to do her schoolwork in the cabin of a boat that was almost as long as her house, with the ocean just outside the portholes and seagulls winging by.

"All right, girls, listen up," Jackie said.

They'd reached the dock by now, and Lily broke out of her daydream and crowded in so she could hear. She didn't want to miss a word.

"We have highly qualified sailing instructors and excellent sailing craft," Jackie said. "Our goal is for you to have the time of your lives while you learn some of the basics of a skill that can bring you a lifetime of pleasure and—in my view—allow you some amazing times for communing with God as well as with your fellow sailors."

I love this, Lily thought. *I just love it. I'm gonna teach the Girlz to sail when we get back home.*

It occurred to her that they were probably disappointed that their cabins didn't get picked for sailing. But at least they were together with one person from their group. She figured she pretty much deserved this.

"However," Jackie was saying, "there is the possibility of danger when you're sailing because you're on the water and the wind can be unpredictable. We can guarantee your safety only if you listen carefully and do exactly as you are told."

All heads nodded.

"All right," Jackie said, "any questions so far?"

"I got one," Maggie said. "What's that stuff on your nose?"

D. J. turned around and gave Maggie an I-can't-believe-you-said-that look.

"It's zinc oxide," Jackie said calmly. "It completely blocks the sun, and I need it because I'm out on the water so much at peak times for ultraviolet rays. And I have had sun poisoning before." She reached into one of the pockets on her vest, which she was wearing over her bathing suit, and pulled out a small tube. "Just to make sure that doesn't happen to anyone else, I'm going to apply some on everybody except Alexandria and D. J."

"I definitely don't want to get sun poisoning," Maggie said. "But just for the record, that stuff is gross!"

Genevieve giggled.

Lily stepped forward and said, "Go ahead. Slap it on me."

Jackie slathered on enough to paint Lily's bedroom, she was sure. When Lily turned around, Maggie burst into hysterical laughter. The rest of them couldn't hold back the giggles either. But it didn't matter. She was going sailing.

Lily did get a little nervous, though, when Jackie said she was going to divide them up. *Please don't let me be with Maggie,* Lily thought. *I won't be able to concentrate.*

Jackie said they would be using two boats. Three of the girls would sail with her, and two would go with Nate, a tanned college-age guy with muscles in his calves that Lily was sure were as hard as boards. They could see him down on the dock, where he was laying out life jackets.

"Genevieve, Alexandria, and Maggie will sail with me," Jackie said, "D. J. and Lily will crew for Nate."

"You mean, we actually get to help sail it?" Maggie said. "We don't have to just sit there and ride?"

"You won't do a whole lot today, but gradually you'll do more. One person *can* sail one of these, but it's much easier with a small crew. Now, girls, our boats are sloops, little daysailers, and they are very stable and steady. They are excellent boats for beginners, but mistakes still count." She looked right at Maggie. "If you have a question that pertains to what you've been asked to do while you're out there, by all means ask it. Otherwise, give it your full concentration."

I will, Lily thought. It was definitely going to be easier without Mag-Pie on her boat.

Lily was the first one to get her life jacket on — though she was so excited her fingers were shaking as she buckled it up — and the first one to board *Francesca,* their trim little sloop.

"She has a yellow hull," Lily said to Nate as D. J. climbed aboard.

"What's a hull?" D. J. said. "Oh — is it okay if I ask that?"

"This bottom part that goes in the water," Lily said. She knew she was sounding a little superior, but Nate smiled at her. She just wanted him to know that she was going to be a very serious sailor.

Nate asked her to hop back up onto the dock and unwrap the ropes — the lines, he called them — from the metal cleats they were tied to, keeping the boat in place.

"Toss them in to D. J. here," he said, "and hop back in."

Lily nodded solemnly and hoisted herself up onto the dock. She could feel the boat lurch beneath her and she mumbled, "Oh, sorry."

That was graceful, she thought. *I'm going to have to work on that.*

She fumbled a lot getting the lines undone. They were wrapped in some weird way that eluded her at first. She glanced up at Nate, who was talking to D. J. Wasn't that just like a man to tie some complicated knot?

"Here you go, D. J.," she said. She tossed the first line to D. J. and scurried to the other cleat. The *Francesca* was already drifting away from the dock on the bow she'd just untied.

She got that one undone more easily and lowered herself into the boat, trying to be graceful about it. She ended up with one leg in the boat and one still up on the dock, stretching into the splits.

I feel like Gumby! she thought. *I'm gonna split in half!*

Nate grabbed her around the waist and pulled her in. She dropped onto the bench seat, already going blotchy in the face.

"Congratulations, Lily," Nate said. "You just cast off the docking lines."

"Oh," Lily said. "I did?"

Nate explained what he was doing as he fiddled with more lines and then took his place at a small wheel near the back of the hull.

"That's the helm!" Lily cried.

She didn't look to see if Nate was impressed this time. The boat was moving as he guided it slowly and carefully clear of the rocky shore, and Lily could hardly breathe.

When he cried out, "Going ahead," he let the two sails rise above them. The boat came alive, and they were suddenly scudding over the tiny white crests and out into the bay. Lily opened her mouth to let out a cry of sheer joy — and had it filled with a shower of salty spray that spewed over D. J. and Lily like a shaken bottle of pop and sent them into shrieks.

"Watch the boom, ladies!" Nate shouted over the wind.

One of the sails swung toward them, and D. J. and Lily ducked as the horizontal pole that held the sail at the bottom grazed over their heads.

45

"I think that was the boom," Lily said to D. J.

After that there was no time to show off what was dancing off the page of that library book and onto the parts of the *Francesca.* It seemed as if Nate were working constantly, first with the sail in the front — which he called the headsail — and then with the one aft, which he told them was the mainsail. The wind on the bay kept him busy, and Lily itched to get her hands on the lines. But she tried to listen as Nate gave them a running commentary on what he was doing — though some of it simply flew away on the breeze.

"We're making leeway — away from the direction of the wind." That felt fun and free and made D. J. gurgle like a water fountain.

"Now I'm going to tack the headsail, so the wind blows on the other side." They both shrieked then as the boat turned and Lily watched more champagne-spray sparkle on D. J.'s face.

"Dead ahead — look astern." D. J. and Lily looked at each other for a blank moment and then whipped their faces to the back of the boat, where the water behind them made two straight lines of bubbles and ripples. "Our wake is dead astern," Nate said.

There was a lot more — talk of sail trimming and steering to windward and even keeling, where the boat felt as if it were going to lie down flat on its side, and the girls had to brace themselves. But after a while, it *all* flew away as Nate pointed out the secret places of the creeks and inlets that fringed the bay and talked about the cats paws — the little waves that formed when the wind blew over a smooth surface. Lily couldn't decide which to daydream about first — sailing into an inlet and finding hidden treasure or being a missionary who sailed to islands to rescue stranded or banished people from starvation. So she was taken by surprise when, as they neared the camp again, Nate said, "Anybody want to take the helm and steer us in?"

"I do!" Lily cried.

Then she looked guiltily at D. J. "Unless you do," she said.

"D. J. can make fast," Nate said. He grinned at her. "Don't worry. I'll tell you what that is."

"Are you gonna tell me what to do with this first?" Lily said, gazing reverently at the wheel.

"It's going to be less windy as we get closer in," Nate said. "That makes steering easier. You're steering to windward."

"Oh," Lily said.

She blinked at him.

"That means you're steering in the direction from which the wind is blowing. The boat wants to steer that way, so you just go with it."

"Oh," Lily said again.

He showed her where to put her hands — and encouraged her to hold on a little more loosely so her knuckles didn't go white.

"Dead ahead," he said. "I'll take over when we get closer to shore. There are a few places where it's easy to run aground — and we *don't* want to do that."

Lily nodded and loosened her grip and looked past the now settling sails to the shoreline ahead. The wind kissed her face, and the boat rose and fell softly on the lazy waves. With a burst of excitement, she suddenly realized — she was sailing.

I've found it! she wanted to shout to God. *You've shown me my thing! I'm supposed to do this in my life!*

She was reluctant to give the helm back over to Nate. She was sure she wouldn't run it aground — how hard could it be to keep the bottom of the boat from getting stuck on the floor of the bay? Even as she slipped back onto her seat, she watched wistfully as D. J. got ready to hop up onto the dock and make fast. She wished she were the one doing it. She wanted to do it all.

Their first sailing adventure was all the Asher girls could talk about that night at supper and even in the cabin before lights out. When they ran out of "Our boat almost keeled over!" and "Did you actually get to drive?" and "That's 'take the helm' in sailing talk," the discussion

47

turned to Nate. Lily deflated a little at that point. Up until then, she'd been talking almost as much as the other girls — except Maggie, who could outtalk an auctioneer. But boys weren't Lily's favorite subject, and she went back to the Girlz Gram she was writing to cheer Suzy up. The poor kid had looked like a prison inmate at dinner.

"So do you think Nate's cute?" D. J. said.

"Of course he's cute," Genevieve said.

Alexandria, of course, nodded. "He's a hottie."

"What's a hottie?" Maggie said.

"Some guy who's hot," D. J. told her.

"What's hot mean?"

Everybody stared at her.

"What?" Maggie said. "I'm just asking for a definition."

Suddenly D. J. burst out laughing. "I don't know!" she said. "It's just what everybody says!"

"I don't know either," Genevieve said. "I never had a boyfriend. Neither has Alexandria."

D. J. nodded. "I like boys — a lot. But I don't go out with anybody." She snorted. "Where are we gonna go?"

She turned to Lily. "How about you?"

"Me?" Lily said. "No! Most of the boys I know are absurd little creeps — I mean, I used to think they were — now there's one I'm friends with, only — I used to hate him, so what do you do with that?"

D. J., Genevieve, and Alexandria nodded sympathetically, and Lily felt herself move closer to them inside — maybe just an inch or two. It surprised her that none of them had ever gone out, even though they were so pretty and popular. Maybe she was more like them than she thought — without the pretty and popular.

Maybe we could be friends, she thought hopefully.

"Hey," Maggie said, poking Lily's bed in that annoying way she did with her fingers. "What's that you're writing?"

Lily looked down at the Girlz Gram and resisted the urge to cover it up with her hands. She could just picture Maggie poking at it any second.

"I'm writing a note to my friend in another cabin," Lily said.

"Oh, yeah — I almost forgot you had only so many friend slots and they're all filled."

Lily could feel the rest of the cabin getting quiet.

"No, I don't," she said, without looking up. "I like everybody — honest."

"Nobody likes absolutely everybody. That's impossible."

Lily could have kissed Jackie for coming in just then and telling them to turn out the lights. As Lily snuggled down into her sleeping bag, she couldn't help but think that Maggie was right. She didn't especially like everybody. She was glad it was D. J. who was her sailing partner — and not Maggie.

Chapter
6

The next day, Lily could barely stand the wait until sailing lessons. She dashed in a little late for breakfast because she stopped off at the post-office window in the canteen to mail the Girlz Gram to Suzy.

Almost everybody was seated by the time she got to the dining hall, and as she passed between the rows of tables to get to the one assigned to Asher cabin, she saw Zooey and — what was the name of that girl she had introduced to Lily? Emily or something? The two of them were leaning their heads together and howling as if neither of them had ever met anyone so funny. Even Suzy was giggling, though she didn't look quite sure what she was laughing at.

For some reason it made Lily's heart sink. It sank even further when she passed the Zebulun table. Kresha was leading most of her cabin mates in a Croatian song that involved hand motions. And Reni — her very best friend in the whole world — had her hands cupped around another African-American girl's ear and was whispering into it. Just the way she always whispered to Lily and nobody else.

What's going on? Lily thought as she took the last few steps to the Asher table. *Are they all just forgetting about me because I'm not with them? I haven't forgotten about them!*

She started to feel the lonely longing for home again. Once more the pancakes looked like circles of cardboard, and the eggs were runny and didn't smell like the ones Mom made.

"Anybody feeling the effects of the sun out there on the water yesterday?" Jackie said.

"Who could?" Maggie said, tapping her nose. "I was wearing a medieval visor, for Pete's sake."

While the rest of the girls quizzed Maggie on what on earth she was talking about this time, Lily had a talk with herself.

There's one thing you can't do at home, Girlz or no Girlz, and that's sail. It's your thing—you know it is. You have to stay here so you can learn to be the best sailor this camp ever trained. Besides, it's the way you're making friends here. It was fun with D. J. yesterday. You two could be sailing buddies—sisters of the sea—

She looked across the table at D. J., who was staring at Maggie as if she'd just grown a second head. When she caught Lily's eye, Lily smiled at her. D. J. darted her eyes to Maggie and back to Lily and grinned. Lily nodded.

Maybe—just maybe—it was going to be all right.

The morning dragged, and quiet time was an entire lifetime. When Jackie came in to remind them to have a few minutes with God, all Lily could see when she closed her eyes were cats paws and white sails and showers of sparkling spray.

Those are God things, she reassured herself. The instant Jackie poked her head in again, Lily was off her bed, swimsuit in hand.

When they walked down to the bay that day, Lily fell into step beside D. J.

"Do you remember all that stuff Nate told us yesterday?" she said.

D. J. shook her head. "I bet you do, though. You're so smart about stuff."

"You made fast, though," Lily said.

D. J.'s brown eyes lit up. "Yeah, I did, didn't I?" She looped her arm through Lily's. "I hope we get to go together again today."

"Why wouldn't we?" Lily said.

D. J. lowered her voice to a husky whisper. "I think I heard Jackie say she was going to switch the teams around today."

"Oh," Lily said.

She barely had a chance to start worrying about it before Jackie stopped them just above the dock. A short, blonde counselor was waiting for them there, sunglasses clipped onto her glasses, smiling a twinkly smile.

"This is Cherie," Jackie said. "She's going to be coaching Lily and, let me see —" Jackie consulted her clipboard. D. J. squeezed Lily's hand. "Lily and Maggie," Jackie said. "D. J., you'll be with the Bobbsey twins and me."

Lily forced herself not to look like she wanted to hurl herself into the bay. As annoying as Maggie was, she didn't want to hurt her feelings. Besides, D. J. was making the best of it, putting an arm around Genevieve's and Alexandria's shoulders. Lily drew the line at hugging Maggie.

"All right, you guys," Cherie said to Lily and Maggie — who were getting their daily dose of zinc oxide, "you ready to go sailing or what?"

She had a friendly New York accent — not like the tough ones Lily sometimes heard on TV — and Lily liked her immediately. She was the one Lily needed to listen to today anyway, not Maggie.

She hurried to keep up with Cherie as she led them briskly down to the *Francesca*.

"She's the one I sailed in yesterday," Lily said. "I got to take the helm for a little while."

"Then you're already an experienced sailor, eh?" Cherie said.

"No!" Lily said. But she smiled with pleasure and thought, *I'm going to be — really fast.*

"You're from upstate New York," Maggie said.

"How'd you guess?" Cherie said.

"You say 'eh' — almost like the Canadians."

"You get around, eh?" Cherie said to her.

Maggie shrugged. "I've been to every continent. Except Antarctica."

"Lucky," Cherie said.

"Yeah — but I never had a best friend."

She said it as casually as if she'd just declared she'd never had caviar. Lily studied her for a second. The concept of not having a best friend was foreign to her. She couldn't even imagine it — at least, not until she came here.

Lily shook herself away from that thought and followed Cherie eagerly down the dock.

"Have a good sail, you guys," D. J. called to them as they passed the *Mermaid.*

"I *will*," Lily said firmly. "Nothing but."

"I'll cast off the docking lines if you want me to," Lily said when they reached the *Francesca.*

"Eager little beaver, aren't ya?" Cherie said. She looked at Maggie. "Did you get to do that yesterday?"

"No," Maggie said.

"Let's let her do it today then," Cherie said to Lily. "Trust me, there's going to be plenty to do."

"That's fine!" Lily said quickly. She didn't want Cherie to think she was anything but a good sport. She wanted everything about this to be perfect.

As they made their way away from the shoreline, Cherie explained a lot of the same things Nate had talked about the day before. Lily watched and listened. At least, she tried to listen.

"Let me tell you how sails work so you can have a picture in your mind," Cherie said. She talked easily while she manned the helm. "Sails extract power from the wind by dividing a stream of air into two paths — shaping both paths into a curve — then allowing them to come together again smoothly."

"So you're talking about the way the sails bend," Maggie said. "I get it. Go on."

Lily didn't, but she nodded anyway.

"The concave side of the sail," Cherie said, making her hand into a cup and pointing to her palm, "is the windward side, and the path of air that flows across it reaches a higher pressure than the flow on the opposite side — the convex side of the sail."

"That would be the leeward side," Maggie said. "Gotcha."

"Except it's pronounced 'loow-rd' side," Cherie said.

"How come?" Maggie said.

"I don't know," Cherie answered.

"There's gotta be a reason — "

"It just *is*!" Lily said. She hoped they could get on with learning how to sail. The instructions were starting to sound kind of hard.

"So the variation in pressure on the two sides," Cherie went on, "is what propels the hull in the water. So it's mostly about controlling the sails, you guys. Basically what you need to know today is that this big pole here is called — "

"The mast," Maggie put in.

"Right. And this is the boom — "

"They almost got hit by that yesterday," Maggie said, nodding at Lily.

"This big line here — " Cherie paused and looked at Maggie.

"You got me," Maggie said.

Cherie grinned. "At last — something you don't already know. That means we're at the right place."

She sure is patient, Lily thought. *I'd have pushed Maggie overboard by now.*

Cherie went on tell them about the various lines, the backstay and the forestay, and the shrouds, which formed diamond shapes on either side of the boat. Cherie showed them a thing that looked like a large, fat, upside-down screw with no point that she called a winch. She said it revolved and helped control the sails. The lines wrapped around it were the halyards that pulled the sails up and held them there.

"I'm going to let you two raise the mainsail and get us pressing on," Cherie said. "I want you to work as a team."

Lily and Maggie both held onto the halyard the way Cherie showed them. Lily wasn't prepared for the way the mainsail suddenly billowed out with air and threatened to pull her and Maggie right out of the boat.

"Got a good gust there, eh?" Cherie cried.

Lily lost her grip on the line. Maggie, who didn't seem at all surprised by the tug, helped Cherie raise the mainsail to the top of the mast and cleat the halyard into place.

"I knew that was coming," Maggie said. "There was more pressure on the windward side. I get it."

I wish I did, Lily thought. *I probably would if she'd just hush up!*

"Now that sail," Cherie said, "is going to flap until we trim it in."

With scissors? Lily thought. *What's she talking about? Just tell me what line to grab and what to do with it!*

"We're going to use these lines to adjust the sail so we stay on an even keel," Cherie said. "Lily — you tighten this one around that cleat."

Lily was able to do that without mishap. Maggie did two others, and Cherie declared the mainsail set.

"The mainsail is set," Lily repeated after her.

"Why'd you do that?" Maggie said.

"Because I just wanted to say it," Lily told her. And then she felt stupid. *I can't let her spoil this for me,* she thought.

"Now we're going to raise the headsail," Cherie said.

She showed them both how to attach the sheets — the lines that controlled the sideways movement of the boat — and tie them on port and starboard, calling out the orders as she continued to steer. Although the bay breeze whipped around the brim of Lily's hat, she was starting to break out into a sweat.

"All right, crew," Cherie said, "haul the halyard and raise the mainsail up the forestay."

"What?" Lily said.

But Maggie was already hauling the halyard line, hand over hand. The headsail flapped noisily.

"Lily! " Cherie said. "Cleat the halyard!"

Maggie poked at Lily with the line and pointed to a cleat. Lily wrapped it around as best she could remember. At least she was doing something instead of feeling stupid.

"All right, crew," Cherie said. "We are fully under sail."

The boat seemed to be moving faster and faster, a fact that delighted Lily as the sails cracked and seagulls screeched out of their way. And then they just seemed to glide for a few minutes, the way a Ferris wheel car floated through the air. Lily closed her eyes to experience it.

"Gotta stay alert," Cherie said. "A changing wind comes along or a couple waves shake us up, and we have work to do."

Maggie was studying the sails. "So the wind isn't just pushing forward — it's lifting up the sails."

"Good!" Cherie said. "And the same thing is happening underneath with the water and the keel. When everything is in balance, we travel in a straight line, like we're doing now. When they're out of balance, the boat turns. Let's upset things so you can see what I mean."

"Upset things?" Lily said. She was kind of enjoying it just the way it was.

"Since you had a little trouble with that line, Lily, I'm going to show Maggie first, and you watch very carefully."

Lily felt her face going blotchy, even in the wind, but she glued her eyes to Cherie as she showed her how to give the boat more and then less sail. She put Lily at the helm. The wheel pulled away from Lily like a stubborn child.

"You've got it," Cherie called out to Maggie. "Look at this — we're accelerating. Now, let me help Lily, here." She got behind Lily and put her arms around her so that she could put her hands on Lily's on the wheel. "You remember me saying that the boat has to be steered in one direction — like this — " she guided the wheel — "to travel in a slightly different direction?"

Lily shook her head.

"That's to get the lift," Maggie said.

"I think I'd do better with the sails," Lily said.

"It's just about time to switch," Cherie said. "Maggie has us in good shape. Let's teach you how to trim the sails and keep us in the groove."

She talked about the angle of the sail meeting the wind and showed Lily how to control that using the sheets — those smaller lines. Lily did exactly what Cherie told her, but the instructions were gone from her head the minute she completed them. Her stomach was starting to churn.

Suddenly the boat began to lean, so that the cats paws were almost within reach.

"All right, ready about!" Cherie called out.

Lily held onto the first thing she could find to keep herself from falling over and looked blankly at Cherie.

"So that means it's time to tack," Maggie said from the helm. "Right?"

"Right — excellent."

Wonderful, Lily thought, *but what does that mean?* She felt herself starting to panic.

"Uncleat the leeward headsail and keep it on the winch, ready to free," Cherie said, as she got busy doing something else.

Lily looked around wildly. Uncleat. She'd done that before. She grabbed a line that was wrapped around something and pulled this way and that until it came loose.

"Are you ready?" Cherie called out.

"Uh-huh," Lily said.

"Then cast off the leeward sheet."

Cast off — Lily thought. *That had to mean let go.*

She opened her hand and the line — the sheet — she was holding flapped out into the wind. In no more than an instant, the boom swung toward her and she ducked, screaming. The *Francesca* lurched sideways, this time so far that Lily saw the mainsail dip the water.

"Haul in the other sheet!" Cherie shouted.

But all Lily could do was grope for a handhold to keep herself on board. It was too late, though. Still grasping for something — anything — Lily felt herself sliding over fiberglass and straight into the bay.

In spite of the life jacket, she went straight down into the salty water. When she came bobbing up, spitting and coughing and flailing, Cherie was beside her, grabbing her from behind and shouting, "Calm down, Lily! Calm down — I've got you!"

Lily looked up, waiting for the whole boat to come crashing down on top of them. But Maggie was tying off lines as if she'd been sailing all her life, and the *Francesca* was once again upright in the water.

"I'm sorry!" Lily cried. "I'm so sorry!"

"Don't worry about it," Cherie said, this time more softly. "Let's just get you back to the dock."

Chapter 7

By the time they'd sailed the little boat back to the dock, Cherie was completely calm.

"Lily, really," Cherie said as she helped her out of the boat, "it happens to the best of us. Don't be discouraged."

Discouraged? Lily wanted to shout at her. *I'm humiliated! I'm devastated! I want to stick my head in a hole and die!*

But Lily muttered a thank you. She was afraid to actually talk. She knew she'd burst into tears, and wouldn't that be just the thing to do in front of Maggie? Lily didn't even look at her. Maggie was sure to be in her face enough later on, asking ten million questions.

Just let me go back to the cabin where I can cry all I want, Lily thought. *In peace.*

But as she turned away from the boat, Lily ran smack into Jackie. Lily didn't have to see Jackie's eyes behind her sunglasses to know she was concerned. It was written into the lines around her mouth.

"What happened?" Jackie said, more to Cherie than to Lily.

"We started to keel," Cherie said. "And Lily took a dive overboard."

We didn't start to keel, Lily thought miserably. *I started to keel. I did keel!*

"Are you all right, Lily?" Jackie said. She slid her sunglasses down to the end of her nose, right over the zinc oxide, and inspected Lily over the top of them.

"I'll be fine if I just go lie down," Lily said.

She was already headed up the dock, but Jackie took hold of her arm.

"This looks like a pretty good cut," she said.

Lily saw for the first time that the back of her right arm was bleeding, right onto her white sailing shorts. *That's okay,* Lily thought. *It's not like I'm ever going sailing again anyway.*

"I have some Band-Aids in my bag," Lily said. "I'll just go put one on —"

"I think we need to have the nurse look at this," Jackie said. "I'll walk you up to the infirmary."

Lily started to protest, but Jackie turned to Cherie and told her to take Maggie back out in the boat. Lily contemplated taking off at a dead run, but Jackie was still holding her arm. She blinked hard to hold back the tears.

The infirmary was on the other side of the dining hall. By the time Lily and Jackie walked there, Lily's tears were all in a lump in her throat. She was working so hard at keeping them there, she forgot she was soaking wet until she went into the room where Jackie told her to wait and heard a voice say, "Lily — why did you go swimming in your shorts?"

To Lily's surprise, it was Zooey, sitting on a bed. Every part of her skin that Lily could see was dotted with something pink and clumpy-looking.

"What are you doing here?" Lily said. She practically ran to Zooey, arms out for a hug.

"Poison ivy," Zooey said.

Lily screeched to a dead halt.

"Yeah, don't touch me," Zooey said. "The way this stuff is oozing, you'd have it in a minute. Plus, you don't want to get calamine lotion all over your shorts." She pulled her head back. "Yikes, Lily, you've already got blood on them. That's never gonna come out."

Lily ignored her and took a few steps closer to study her rash. She was definitely covered with it, and most of it was swollen and angry looking. Even her face was red and puffy.

"What did you do, roll around in it?" Lily said.

"I don't know," Zooey said. "I didn't even know it was there! Our cabin went on a hike yesterday. It was so awesome, Lily. We stood on top of this one cliff, and we could see you guys down there sailing — anyway, then we went into a woods, and I guess that's where I got it." She looked ruefully at her polka-dotted arms. "Nobody else in our cabin got it, except Emmy a little bit. But hers doesn't look this bad."

Lily saw Zooey's eyes start to fill up, and, poison ivy or not, she sat down on the bed next to her.

"I'm sorry, Zooey," she said. "Does it hurt that bad?"

"It's not that! The nurse says I'm having an allergic reaction to it, and I might need to go home and be treated by a doctor." Zooey's voice rose to a mini-wail. "I don't want to go home! I'm having fun here!"

"Are you?" Lily said. "Are you really?"

"I love the girls in my cabin — and they even like *me!* — and we're having so much fun. I'll freak if I have to leave, Lily!"

It was all Lily could do not to cry out, "Then I'll go home for you, and you stay here! I'll even take your poison ivy!" As it was, she did say, "I'd go with you if I could, Zooey."

"Lily?" Jackie said from the doorway. "Let's have the nurse look at that arm."

During the ten steps it took to get to the examining room, Lily came up with an entire scenario of having to have stitches ... no, maybe even plastic surgery on her arm and having to go home right away ... and being advised by her doctor never to go to summer camp again.

But Nurse Nancy — that was her real name — cleaned up the cut with an antibiotic ointment, put a big, square Band-Aid on it, and told her she would be as good as new for sailing the next afternoon. Lily bit her lip to keep from saying, "Are you sure? I'd like a second opinion."

The camp was still quiet as Jackie walked with Lily down the path toward Asher cabin.

"You can go back to the girls," Lily said. "I'll be fine."

"Will you?"

Lily looked up in surprise. Jackie had taken off her sunglasses and was chewing on the earpiece and watching Lily as she walked.

"Yeah," Lily said. "She told us it wasn't that bad."

"I'm not talking about your cut. I'm talking about you." Jackie put her arm around Lily's shoulder. She smelled like sunscreen and salt water and hot skin. "I know you aren't happy here. Is there anything I can do to help you?"

The tears in Lily's throat took that as permission to burst out in one big sob. Jackie tightened her arm on Lily's shoulder and gave her a chance to get a few more sobs out so she could talk.

"I feel like I'm so different from the other girls in the cabin," Lily said finally. "I'm sure they all think I'm a nerd and a creep, except for Maggie — she just thinks I'm a snob, although after today — anyway, most of the time I just don't fit in — not like I do with my own Girlz. See — I came up here with my four best friends — we're the Girlz Only Club."

"I know about the Girlz," Jackie said. "I saw it on your registration form."

Please don't tell me I'm here to make more friends, Lily thought as she smeared the tears off of her face with the back of her hand. *I can't handle that right now.*

But Jackie was quiet for a few minutes as they started down the last hill to the cabin. Then she said, "How is it with you and the Girlz? How is it different than it is with the girls in the cabin?"

Lily didn't even hesitate. She'd been thinking about almost nothing else since the first day.

"I'm like the leader of the Girlz," she said. "I think of cool things for us to do — and then we all help each other and accept each other for exactly who we are. See, Reni is a leader too, but she's sometimes kind of abrupt, so we help her not to be so — "

"Let's stay focused on you for now," Jackie said.

They'd reached the cabin by then, and Jackie motioned for Lily to sit on the little step with her. Lily stifled a moan. Would this woman never just leave her alone?

"I have three assignments for you, Lily," Jackie said when they were seated.

Lily grunted. "Study up on sailing is probably one of them. I was such a geek out there today."

Jackie held up a tanned hand — and seemed to be holding back a smile. "I didn't say guess what assignments I have for you, did I?"

"Oh," Lily said. "No. Sorry."

Jackie shook her head, grinning now. "You're a piece of work, aren't you, girl?"

"I guess," Lily said. She wasn't sure what that was. Right now she was certain it couldn't be good.

"All right, first of all," Jackie said, holding up one finger, "I want you to have some quiet time alone with God every day. Not just the fifteen minutes I ask everybody to do at quiet time, but some real alone time."

"I do that at home!" Lily said. "I never miss a night. But here, it's kinda hard."

"Of course it is, because you're never by yourself. If you can't stay awake after the other girls are asleep — in which case you can do the flashlight under the covers thing — I can wake you up, say, twenty minutes before the other girls and you can do it then. I'll even let you go outside."

"You would?" Lily said. "Totally alone?"

Jackie nodded. "I think you're the kind of girl who needs that."

"I *so* do!"

She was about to launch into a description of how hard it was to find that at home too, what with Joe and Art and Tessa—but Jackie put up a second finger. "Second—I want you to concentrate on serving the other girls in the cabin in every way you can. Your alone time and the individual activities we do in Bible study are for you to think about *you*. The rest of the time, I want you to think about how you can serve *them*, no matter what."

"I've done that before," Lily said. "This last winter, when Suzy and I were in a speech contest and it got kind of ugly, I had to concentrate on serving." She could feel her brow furrowing into lines of freckles. "But that was easy because they were my friends. I don't think the girls in our cabin are gonna want me serving them."

She could imagine Genevieve and Alexandria looking down in disgust as she scurried to pick up their dirty clothes—or D. J. saying, "Thanks, Lily, but that's okay—I can put my own toothpaste on my toothbrush."

"I think you're wrong," Jackie said, "but if it makes it easier for you, do it without their knowing that you're serving them."

"Like in secret, you mean?" Lily said.

"Something like that."

Lily considered that. It might be fun—although it would be more fun with her own Girlz.

"Third," Jackie said. She poked up one more finger. "I want you to participate in absolutely everything that goes on in the cabin and with the girls—every discussion, every pillow fight. You don't have to be the leader. You don't even necessarily have to say something every time. But I want you there, involved."

Lily looked at her helplessly.

"That one won't be easy for you, I see," Jackie said.

"I don't think so," Lily said. But she knew there was no point in arguing with Jackie. No college student counselor would have been *this* tough.

"I tell you what," Jackie said. She glanced at her watch. "The girls won't be back for another twenty minutes. Why don't you use this as your first quiet time? Go in — get showered and changed — and then talk to God. How does that sound?"

"I thought you'd never ask," Lily said. She was practically in the shower before Jackie got to the main path.

She expected to cry in the shower, but by the time she was standing under the water, she was more mad than sad.

I'm gonna feel worse than ever, she thought. She could just see D. J. and Genevieve starting a pillow fight and Alexandria joining in — all three of them laughing and howling. And then Lily would toss a pillow, and it would knock Alexandria out or explode in Genevieve's face — and then D. J. would say something like, "It's okay, Lily, it could have happened to one of us," when she knew good and well it couldn't because they weren't ridiculous nerds!

Lily felt a little guilty when she sat down on her bed, clean and dry. She hadn't thought about God once the whole time in the shower, and that was what she was supposed to be doing. But even as she opened her Talking-to-God Journal, all she could think about was writing a letter to Mom and Dad, asking them if she could just come home.

You don't even have to come get me, she decided she would write. *I'll take a bus home. I'll hitchhike!*

But Lily slapped the journal closed. She knew they wouldn't come get her even if she begged them. They were very big on making her finish the things she started — probably because she started so many things.

The only way they would let me come home, she thought, *would be if I got sick like Zooey.*

The thought brought her straight up on the bed. How hard could it be to get poison ivy? Zooey had done it without even knowing.

Lily looked at her watch. She still had ten minutes. If she could find a patch of it fast, she could be infected by the time the girls got back from sailing — itching by lights out — and on her way home tomorrow.

Sticking her journal under her mattress, Lily padded quietly out of the cabin — as if there were anyone there to hear her — and crept down the path and off into the wooded area. So far, so good. The next step was to find some poison ivy.

Leaves of three, let it be, she thought. She'd heard that somewhere, though until now she'd never really considered what it meant.

"I guess it means three leaves in a bunch," she muttered to herself. And it had to be down on the ground for Zooey to have gotten it all over her like that. She'd never known Zooey to climb a tree.

She's really into this whole camp thing, Lily thought. *Who'd have thought she'd like it more than I do? Although that wouldn't actually take much.*

She stopped in a spot where three trees stood close together. The entire ground under them was one big fluffy bed of three-leafed plants. Lily squatted down to inspect them.

Yeah, there were three leaves, all right. They weren't necessarily the same size, but they sure looked wicked. Lily touched one with her finger and looked at her skin. Then she snorted.

Did I expect to break out in hives immediately? she thought.

No, tonight would be soon enough. And she was going to need more than a tiny rash.

Taking a deep breath, Lily turned around and let herself fall into the plant bed. It gave softly beneath her, and she moved her arms and

66

legs the way she did when she was making snow angels in the winter. The plants smelled damp and pleasantly musty. If she hadn't been on a mission, she was sure she would have enjoyed it. But with her goal in mind, she flipped over onto her stomach and let the leaves touch her face and her neck and the fronts of her arms.

And then she just lay there, the sun dappling down on her through the trees, the moist smell filling up her head, the prayer taking up all her thoughts. *God, please, please let me go home — and don't ever let me leave there again.*

But it wasn't a comforting prayer — not as she thought about her family leaving home for a whole year to go to England. And what about after that? She'd always dreamed of going away to college and then traveling the whole world — even Africa.

No, she thought, *I'm gonna have to stay home forever, because that's the only place where I can be me.*

"Hey," said a voice above her. "What are you doing?"

Before Lily could roll over and answer, another body plopped down next to her. Lily opened one eye.

It was Maggie.

Chapter 8

Lily opened her other eye. Maggie was directly in her face, blinking curiously behind her wire-rimmed glasses.

Can't a person even get poison ivy in peace? Lily thought. She groaned and turned over. Maggie settled in cozily beside her.

"What are you doing?" Maggie said.

"Lying here," Lily said.

"Because?"

Because if I don't go home I'm going to go bonkers! Lily wanted to scream at her. *So leave me alone!*

But she could still hear Jackie's words ringing in her ears, telling her to serve the girls in the cabin. *Not* telling Maggie to get lost was the only thing she could think of at the moment. So instead, she said, "What are *you* doing here?"

"Looking for you," Maggie said. "Everybody else is doing other stuff. It's free time."

"Oh, yeah," Lily said. She closed her eyes. Maybe if Maggie thought she was asleep she'd leave.

No such luck.

"You missed a great sail," Maggie said. "I'm thinking my

parents really messed up when they wouldn't let me help on that cruise. Cherie says I'm a natural sailor."

Lily could feel her heart sagging. The very words she had hoped — expected! — to hear herself had been bestowed on Maggie.

"I tacked, like, three times," Maggie was going on. "Cherie says she never had anybody take to it like I did."

"That's really good," Lily said. She knew it was a stingy compliment, but she felt lucky to be able to choke out that much. *She's throwing it in my face!* Lily thought. *She's throwing it right in my face!*

Maggie sat up and arranged herself cross-legged, looking down at Lily with interest.

"Do you feel dumb now?" she said. "You know, since you just about keeled the boat over?"

"Yes," Lily said, gritting her front teeth.

"Well, you shouldn't. Not everybody can do everything."

Lily stared at her. Maggie just chattered on.

"It's like I'm pretty good at everything when it comes to school, except for biology. I stink at that. I can't stand cutting open frogs and stuff. I just know I'm going to get a disease, even though they're in formaldehyde and all. If I can't do biology, it's going to totally blow my plan to be an astronaut and study other planets from a space station, because you have to be good in all the sciences. I try, but it just doesn't come naturally to me."

If it really did bother Maggie, Lily sure couldn't see it. Maggie plucked a leaf and began to happily dissect it.

Why would it bother her? Lily thought. *So she can't poke at frog guts — what difference does that make here?*

Lily sighed as she watched Maggie pick off another leaf from the soft bed they were sitting in and hold it up to the sun to examine it. How on earth was she supposed to serve somebody whose only need seemed to be a cure for her fear of sudden illness?

"I wonder if these are any good to eat," Maggie said as she regarded the leaf.

That's when it came to Lily.

"Don't, Maggie!" she said. "That's poison ivy!"

Maggie froze with her mouth already open. She gazed in horror at the leaf that was still pressed between her fingers.

"I forgot I was even in it," Lily said, "or I would've told you."

Maggie shook the leaf away from her fingers and jerked to her feet in one large spasm. Stepping frantically from foot to foot, she screamed and smacked at her skin as if she were swatting away bees.

"It's going to eat away my skin!" she cried. "It's going to eat it right off!"

"Are you allergic to it?" Lily said.

Maggie paused in the middle of the panic dance and stared at Lily. "Can you *be* allergic to it? Oh, no! I could go into anaphylactic shock! I could die!"

For someone who's going to die, Lily thought, *she sure isn't too eager to get away from what is supposedly killing her.* She was still stomping around ankle deep in the bed of poison ivy.

"Okay, come on," Lily said. She was standing up by now, and she reached out and grabbed one of Maggie's flying wrists. "I'll take you to Jackie."

Maggie seemed only a little comforted by that, and she continued to bellow as Lily led her out of the poison ivy patch and down the path to the cabin. When Lily called out for Jackie, D. J. poked her head out and said she wasn't there.

"Tell her I took Maggie to the nurse, okay?" Lily said.

By then Alexandria and Genevieve joined D. J. in the doorway, drawn, Lily was sure, by Maggie's carrying on.

"I almost *ate* it!" was Maggie's chorus now. "I could have gotten it all down my throat — into my esophagus!"

Lily took Maggie by both shoulders from behind and steered her ahead.

"I think I'm having trouble breathing," Maggie said. "I really think I am!"

She seemed to be breathing well enough to keep that up, so Lily continued to push her in front of her until they got to the infirmary. Nurse Nancy met them at the door, probably having heard Maggie all the way from the dining hall, Lily was sure.

"She sat in some poison ivy," Lily said to the nurse.

"Some?" Maggie cried. "There was a whole *bed* — and I laid down in it! I almost ate it, even!"

Nurse Nancy nodded calmly and steered her toward the examining room. "Why don't you go in and say good-bye to Zooey," she said to Lily, nodding toward the room with the bed.

"Good-bye!" Lily said. "Is she really leaving?"

Nurse Nancy didn't answer as she closed the examining room door behind her and Maggie, whose cries obviously drowned Lily — and everything else — out completely.

Lily hurried into the room where she'd last left Zooey. She was lying down on the bed, face so swollen her hazel eyes were in slits. Lily couldn't tell if it was from poison ivy or from crying. Her duffel bag and backpack were next to the door.

"They're making me go home, Lily," she said — instead of "hello." "I don't want to go home!"

"Are you in anafala — some kind of shock?" Lily said.

"Huh?"

"Can you breathe?"

"Yes, I can breathe! I want to stay in camp, Lily! My cabin needs me!"

Lily sat down on the edge of the bed and put her hand on Zooey's arm.

"Don't touch me!" Zooey said.

71

Lily yanked her hand back. "I'm sorry," she said. "Did I hurt you?"

"No — I just don't want you to get it. I'm totally contagious."

Lily shook her head. "Don't worry about it. I just rolled in a whole patch of it on purpose."

"Why did you do that?" Zooey said. "Do you want to end up like me?"

"Yes," Lily said. "As a matter of fact, I do. That way I could go home with you."

Zooey struggled to smile. "That's so sweet of you, Lily," she said. "It *is* gonna be totally boring back in Burlington with everybody else still up here. But you gotta stay here and have fun."

Lily didn't have the heart to tell her that wasn't what she'd meant, and she ducked her head so Zooey wouldn't read it in her eyes. She was glad that Nurse Nancy picked that moment to come in with Maggie.

"Why don't you have a seat, Maggie?" she said. "Come on, Zooey — the medicine has come in from town. I need to give you a shot, girl."

"Good-bye, Lily," Zooey said tearfully.

"Bye," Lily said. She could hardly hold back the tears herself. When Zooey and the nurse were gone, she had to swallow down a big lump.

"I'm going to be okay," Maggie said — as if Lily had asked. "She doesn't see any signs of an allergic reaction yet, but she wants me to sit here for a while so she can observe me."

"That's good," Lily said, edging toward the door.

"Aren't you gonna stay here with me?" Maggie said.

It wasn't one of her I'm-now-going-to-dig-into-your-business questions. She actually seemed a little anxious.

"Sure," Lily said. She dropped into a chair next to her.

"I heard what you said to that girl," Maggie said.

"Zooey."

"Yeah—you told her you wished you could go home with her."

Lily shrugged. She didn't feel like pretending it wasn't true.

"I don't want you going home," Maggie said. "You're the only person in this whole camp I relate to."

She then immediately turned her attention to her arms, which she examined minutely. Lily was sure if there had been a magnifying glass or a microscope handy, she would have used it.

She "relates" to me, Lily thought. *Does that mean she likes me or something?*

It was supposed to be a compliment, she was pretty sure. But Maggie wasn't like the Girlz. She asked nosy questions and said things she obviously didn't think about before she said them—or after she said them, for that matter—and she was so hysterical about getting a germ or a rash, she hadn't once seemed to remember that Lily had been lying in the bed of poison ivy right beside her.

And I'm supposed to serve her, Lily thought. *So since she "relates" to me, that means I've gotta hang out with her?*

At the moment, with Maggie staring at her knees as if she were going to pounce on the first bump that erupted, Lily decided that was a pretty big sacrifice.

Nurse Nancy let Maggie go at suppertime, and she and Lily hurried to join the line outside the dining hall. Suzy was dangling alone at the end of it. She looked even more miserable than she had before, if that were possible.

"I miss Zooey so much," she said as Lily hugged her. "I can't stand it without her. I wish I could be with you."

Lily didn't have a chance to comfort her because Suzy's counselor came to collect her. When she was gone, Maggie said, "Wow—that Zooey must be a miracle person or something, the way you all can't deal with it when she isn't around."

"She's not a miracle person," Lily said, lips tight. "She's our friend. We'd feel that way no matter which one of us had to leave."

73

"Oh, yeah, your little group," Maggie said.

Lily listened for a trace of nastiness in Maggie's voice, ready to jump on it—serving or no serving. But Maggie seemed to be considering the matter the way she did just about everything else.

"I don't know about stuff like that," she said finally. "I don't have that many friends. And the ones I have sure don't cry when I leave." She shrugged. "My mother doesn't even cry when I leave."

Lily looked at her quickly, in time to see a little sadness cross her face.

After the usual riot of beach balls and praise songs at that night's group meeting, Mary Francis gave a talk Lily missed most of. Her mind drifted off to the way things were falling apart again. After her first day of sailing, she'd thought maybe camp would be worth sticking with after all. But after today, even that was all messed up. She doubted Jackie and Cherie and Nate would even let her in another boat.

And now that Maggie's my sailing partner, she thought, *I'm stuck serving her all the time.*

Maggie hadn't left her side since they were in the infirmary. It was definitely better not feeling like she was always alone. But if it weren't for the serving thing, Lily knew she might be trying to shake her.

It's not that I don't like her, Lily thought. *But I don't think I would have picked her for my friend.*

They all went back to their cabins earlier than usual that night to do their activity. Jackie got the Asher girls settled in a circle on the ends of beds and on the floor and told them what was up.

"I want each one of you to tell something about yourself that you don't especially like or that you'd like to work on," she said.

I could be here for days, Lily thought.

"Then we're going to work with each one of you," Jackie said, "on accepting that quality or issue or whatever it is tonight and praying for your growth in it tomorrow. Remember what Mary Francis just said: we must be where we are but also be willing to move ahead."

Lily looked at Genevieve and Alexandria and D. J., who all had their brows wrinkled into rows as if they were thinking hard.

I bet this is hard for them, Lily thought. *There's nothing wrong with them!*

For her part, she was having trouble picking just one. She was glad Jackie didn't ask her to go first again. She didn't have a chance because D. J. dove right in.

"I *know* what I don't like about myself," she said. "I'm always getting in trouble for stuff at home — you know, like because I knock things over when I'm in a hurry or I get excited and blurt out stuff at the table."

"You're lively, D. J.," Jackie said. "It's part of your charm."

D. J. shook her head, her short dark bangs ruffling across her forehead. "My parents don't think it's all that charming when I break a lamp. My sister never breaks anything."

"Is she a baby?" Maggie said.

"No — she's two years older than me, and she never does anything wrong. I mean *anything.*"

"Does she ever get out of bed?" Lily said.

"Huh?" D. J. said.

Lily shifted, her face starting to blotch. But Jackie had told her to participate. "My mom says if you get out of bed in the morning, you're bound to make some kind of mistake during the day."

"Valerie gets out of bed," D. J. said. "And she goes out and is Miss Everything. Plus, she's beautiful. Beautiful *and* good. Sometimes I think maybe my parents wish I was more like her."

"That's where you are today," Jackie said. "Girls, let's pray that D. J. can accept that for now, and that tomorrow God will show her a different way."

Wow, Lily thought when all heads were bowed, if D. J. thinks she isn't as good as her sister, Valerie must be amazing.

They moved on around the cabin from there. Genevieve said what she didn't like about herself was that she wanted to spend time talking to God and all that, but she didn't know how, and when she did try something, God never talked back. Lily was surprised that Genevieve even thought about things like that. She'd never heard of a pretty, popular girl who cared about God.

But Alexandria surprised her even more.

"I go totally shy when Genevieve's not with me," she said. "I love her, but I don't like it that I freak out if we're not together. Like — "

She looked at Genevieve, who started to open her mouth. But Jackie whispered, "You tell it, Alexandria."

Alexandria looked at her pink-painted toenails, and her tanned shoulders drooped as she talked. "My mom sent in a letter with our registration, saying that if I wasn't in a cabin with Genevieve, I wouldn't come."

I wish I'd come up with that, Lily thought. But somehow it didn't settle just right.

The girls and Jackie all prayed for Alexandria. Then Maggie took her turn.

"I don't like it that I disappoint my parents sometimes," she said.

"Could you be a little more specific?" Jackie said.

"It's mostly when my grades aren't good. They want straight A's, and I still get some A-minuses, mostly because I miss school a lot being sick. I get everything that comes along." She glanced down at her arms. "I thought I'd be swollen up from poison ivy by now, but I don't even have a rash yet."

"Poison ivy?" Jackie said. "Where on earth would you have picked that up?"

"Right out there," Maggie said, pointing to the window.

Lily started to squirm.

"I don't think there's any poison ivy on the campgrounds, "Jackie said. "They're very careful to keep it under control. You might pick some up on a hike if you left camp, but —"

"No, there's an entire patch of it right up the path," Maggie said. "Lily and I were laying in it this afternoon."

Jackie's eyes traveled slowly to Lily, who could feel her blotches growing together. Although Jackie gave her a pointy-eyed look, she just said, "Let's pray for Maggie."

When they'd done that, Jackie said, "Looks like it's your turn, Lily."

Once again, all Lily's experience speaking in front of groups seemed to seep out through the tiny holes in the screens. Everyone else had been so honest and yet none of their issues had made them seem half as bad as she felt about herself right now. How could she say, *The one of about a hundred things I don't like about myself is that I want to go home!* It sounded stupid.

"Can't you think of anything you want to change about yourself?" Maggie said.

"No!" Lily said. "I mean yes!" She wanted to crawl under the bed. Now they were all going to think she was conceited. Why did Maggie have to ask so many questions? Lily groped for something — anything. She spit out the first thing that came to her.

"I don't like it that I stink at sailing. I really thought it was going to be my thing."

It was quiet in the cabin, so quiet that Lily was sure she could hear Jackie's thoughts: *You're supposed to participate, Lily. Is that lame contribution really participating?*

"Then it's just like I thought at first," D. J. said. "You *are* perfect, Lily. Just like my sister."

"I don't think I'm perfect!" Lily said. She was sure she was now one big blotch from head to toe.

"You might not *think* you are," D. J. said, "But you just about are. I thought it the first day."

"I started thinking it the day we did our collages," Genevieve said. "I thought, man, this girl does everything and looks totally cute while she's doing it."

"Well, nobody's exactly perfect," Maggie said.

Jackie held up her hand. "All right. Let's sort this out," she said. "Lily, you're used to doing everything well that you try, is that right?"

"Well, yeah," Lily said. "My mom always says I go at everything 150 percent or 200 percent — it goes up every time I try something new."

"Oh, so I get it." It was Alexandria. "What you don't like about yourself right now is that you can't be perfect at everything."

"That's funny," D. J. said, "'cause that's what I've been starting to like about you. At first, I thought you were so perfect you were too good for me."

"No!" Lily said.

Alexandria and Genevieve looked at each other. "That's what *we* thought," Genevieve said.

"But I'm *so* not perfect!" Lily said.

Maggie grunted. "Just because you keeled over the sailboat?"

"Not just that," Lily said. She looked at their faces. No mouths were smirking. No eyes were rolling. But still, it was hard to say what she would already have blurted out to the Girlz. "You aren't kidding?" she said.

They shook their heads. Lily closed her eyes for a second — and then plunged.

"See — from the first minute, I figured you guys were so perfect, I wasn't gonna fit in."

"No way I'm perfect," D. J. said. "When nobody's looking, I pick my nose."

"That's nothing," Genevieve said. "Me and Alexandria call our principal's kid 'Lover Lips' behind his back because he's always trying to get girls to kiss him."

"Gross me out and make me icky!" Lily said.

"'Gross me out and make me icky'?" D. J. said. She let out a hoot. "I love that!"

"I'm going to start saying that," Genevieve said.

"Me too," Alexandria said. Then she put her hand up to her mouth.

"What?" Maggie said.

"I should think of something different," she said. "I mean, if I'm trying to stop being Genevieve's clone." She looked around helplessly. "But what would I say?"

They were deep in the throes of trying to come up with a good phrase for Alexandria, with Lily offering the best-liked one so far — "*That* is so *foul!*" — when Jackie dropped four bags of mini candy bars on the floor in front of them.

"To celebrate cabin bonding," she said. "By the way, be thinking of a name for our group. Just plain 'Asher' doesn't fit us."

Lily split open a bag of Three Musketeers bars and looked up at the group. "I have one I thought of out on the boat the first day,' she said. "We don't have to use it, if you don't want — "

"Yeah, yeah, we know," Maggie said. "What is it?"

"How about 'Sisters of the Sea'?" Lily said. "If you think it's stupid, just tell me."

"I love it!" D. J. said. "It sounds like we're mermaids."

"Or widows of sailors lost at sea," Genevieve said.

"Why, Genevieve," Jackie said. "How romantic."

D. J. raised a hand to high-five Lily. "Good call," she said. "You rock!"

Lily let a grin spread across her face. "You guys rock too," she said.

There was a tap on the screen, but they all ignored it except Jackie, who slipped out the door. A circle had formed that nobody seemed to want to break, lest this magic mood should pass.

"I'm really not perfect," Lily said to the faces that were now starting to look different to her. "Sometimes I get so frustrated with my little brother, I tell him to shut up."

"That's all?" D. J. said. "You're nice! I—"

"Lily?" Jackie said from the doorway. "Could we speak with you for a minute?"

Lily scrambled from her perch on her bed beside Maggie.

"Don't say anything fun until I get back," she said to the group.

Outside the screen door, Jackie was on the steps. Mary Francis was standing there too, her white hair shining like a halo in the cabin's light. Lily felt butterflies waking up in her stomach.

"Hi, Lily," Mary Francis said. "We have a situation you might be able to help us with."

"Me?" Lily said.

"Yes," she said. "It's about Suzy Wheeler."

Chapter 9

Lily's butterflies went into a frenzy.

"Suzy?" she said. "Is she okay?"

Mary Francis gave a faint smile. "*She* doesn't think she's okay. Now, Lily, before I ask you this, I want you to know that you do *not* have to agree to it. It's entirely up to you."

"Okay," Lily said. "What is it?"

"Ever since Zooey left this afternoon," Mary Francis said, "Suzy has been inconsolable. She cried so hard after supper her counselor brought her to me because she was afraid she was going to make herself sick." Mary Francis gave a soft smile. "Most cases of homesickness work themselves out in a day or two, but once in a while, we come across one that isn't going to make it through the session if we don't do something. I think that's our Suzy."

"I could talk to her," Lily said. "I was homesick myself until just tonight, and I think I'm over it."

Jackie and Mary Francis exchanged grown-up looks. "I'm glad to hear that, Lily," Mary Francis said. "You keep that in mind as you think about this. Now that Zooey has gone home, there's an empty space in Suzy's cabin. She asked if you could move into it.

It's entirely up to you. We don't usually do this, but in Suzy's case, it might help."

"But only if it's what *you* want to do," Jackie said. "It would mean you'd have to switch from sailing to hiking."

Lily looked from one of them to the other and then down at her nails.

Two hours ago, she wouldn't even have had to stop and think about it. To be with one of her Girlz *and* escape the humiliation of another sailing lesson? She'd have been kissing Mary Francis's feet.

But now she wasn't quite sure. They might be starting to like her in Asher cabin. They at least liked it that she wasn't perfect, because neither were they. She was laughing with them and even starting to trust that they weren't going to treat her like she was an alien. She was one of the Sisters of the Sea.

Lily looked up to see Mary Francis watching her.

"I want to help Suzy," Lily said. "I kind of know how she feels."

"Kind of?" Jackie said.

"Okay — so I *really* know how she feels. And she *is* one of my best friends." Lily stopped.

"I hear a 'but' in your voice," Mary Francis said.

"Yeah," Lily said. "I made some promises to Jackie about our cabin."

"Ah." Mary Francis folded her hands at her waist, the way she always did when she was about to give the girls a spiritual direction. "Sounds like you don't know exactly what to do right now."

"I don't," Lily said. And, she thought to herself, *Mary Francis doesn't know the half of it.* Sure, she was just starting to feel comfortable with her cabin mates, but it would be so much easier to go live with Suzy and be her Lily-the-Leader self again. She knew how to do that.

But somehow that didn't feel right. Once again, it wouldn't settle.

"Tell you what let's do," Mary Francis said. "Why don't we wait for your answer in the morning? That will give you some time to talk to God about it."

"I'll arrange for some of that alone time we talked about," Jackie said.

Lily asked if she could write Suzy a note. Mary Francis said yes, and Lily hurried into the cabin to get a Girlz Gram and a pen. When she opened the screen door, Maggie and D. J. tumbled forward. Genevieve and Alexandria were at one of the windows, looking like they'd just sneaked into the movies without tickets.

"Hel-lo-o!" Lily said. "You were *so* listening!"

"We couldn't hear that much," Maggie said. "You should've talked louder."

"It really wasn't any of our business," Genevieve said.

D. J. cocked her head at Lily. "It is kind of our business if you're gonna move out of our cabin — I mean, after you named us and stuff."

"I didn't say I was moving out," Lily said.

Maggie's eyes narrowed behind her glasses. "But you didn't say you weren't, either."

"I have to give Mary Francis a note," Lily said.

She avoided all four pairs of eyes as she dug out a Girlz Gram form and a pen, but she took it outside to write on it. She couldn't think straight with all of them watching her.

After she scribbled out a note to Suzy saying something vague about everything being all right and having sweet dreams and talking to her tomorrow, she handed the Girlz Gram to Mary Francis and followed Jackie back into the cabin. The girls were a little quicker this time. They were all on their beds, studying their toenails or pretending to be asleep when Jackie squeaked the screen door open. Lily could feel the tension, as if someone had sprayed it into the air out of a can.

I wish Mary Francis hadn't even come here, Lily thought, as she followed Jackie into her little nook. *Things were finally starting to go good.*

But as Jackie closed the door and left Lily there alone, she felt a pang of guilt as she sank into the pillows on Jackie's bed.

What about Suzy? She's one of my best friends! I can't just leave her alone to be miserable just because I've made other friends. She wouldn't do that to me.

And yet Reni had, Lily thought. *And so had Zooey and Kresha.*

They had all made new friends here at camp. Lily herself was just beginning to, and it felt good.

Lily hugged one of Jackie's pillows and looked glumly out into the silhouettes of the trees hovering at the edges of the path. *I don't love Reni any less because I'm making friends with D. J. and them,* she thought. *I don't even love Suzy less.*

It was so confusing, and there was no one to ask. She knew what the girls in the cabin would say, and Jackie too. If she could, she would ask Mom or Dad — or even Art. But they were so far away.

A wave of homesickness started to sweep over her, and Lily realized she hadn't felt that in a couple of hours. It was fresh now, and it hurt.

Who's gonna help me with this? she whispered.

Who do you think? her thoughts whispered back.

Mary Francis had said she should talk to God about it. Jackie had made her promise to talk to him at least once a day. Why was it so hard here at camp?

Because I don't have China and Otto, Lily told herself. *Because I'm not in my room. Because I thought they'd make fun of me writing in a journal, like God could really read it. But he can! He knows what I'm gonna write while I'm writing it.*

Lily stopped and tossed the pillow away from her. "Well, du-uh," she said out loud. "I don't really *have* to write it."

Of course she'd prayed without her journal before — but not when she was alone like this, trying to figure something out. She wasn't quite sure what to do. But that wasn't new. Ever since she'd been at Camp

Galilee her usual way of doing just about everything seemed to be missing. It was as if she'd forgotten to pack it in her duffel bag.

Lily retrieved the pillow and buried her face in it as she began to talk. "God," she said into the down, "why did you send me to camp? To take care of Suzy, or to serve the girls in the cabin like Jackie said? If you tell me that, I'll know what to do."

God didn't exactly tell her. *He probably didn't have a chance,* she thought later. It felt so good to be talking to him, she didn't stop there. God got an earful about how homesick she was and how much she wanted to be good at sailing and how happy she was to finally be kind of accepted in the cabin. And how much she hated the scrambled eggs in the dining hall. She fell asleep before she got to the Amen.

When Jackie woke her up the next morning, the other girls were going out the door to breakfast.

"I had a talk with them last night, so they understand the position you're in a little better," she said, "but I still thought you might need some separation from them until you talk to Suzy."

Lily picked the sticky sleep out of her eyes. "I still don't know what I'm going to say to her."

"Then I think you should wait until after today's Bible study to tell her anything."

"Why?" Lily said.

"I think you'll see," Jackie said.

Lily pulled her clothes on, scooped her red curls into a scrunchie, and hurried with Jackie to the dining hall. Most of the crowd had already gone in. Suzy was hanging out near the door.

"Take a few minutes," Jackie said. "I'll save you some eggs."

Goody, Lily thought. She felt as if her feet weighed a ton apiece as she went toward Suzy.

Suzy waited until Jackie had disappeared inside the dining hall before she flung herself at Lily. Her eyes were puffy, but they were expectant. Lily hugged her hard so she wouldn't have to look at her.

"When are you moving in?" Suzy said. "Your bed's right next to mine."

"I don't know if I am yet," Lily said. "I have to wait until after Bible study."

Suzy wriggled away from her. Her puffy eyes pinched down into slits.

"Why?" she said. "Why aren't they letting you come?"

"It isn't them," Lily said. "It's up to me, and I have to wait."

"But we could be together!" Suzy's eyes were no longer expectant. They were cloudy with anger. "I thought I was your best friend next to Reni—just like you're mine next to Zooey!"

"I am—you are!" Lily said.

"Well, you sure don't act like it. I hate it here so much I can hardly stand it—and you could make it better just like that—" Suzy snapped her fingers. "And you won't!"

"I didn't say I wouldn't—I just have to wait—"

"What difference does it make?"

"Girls," said a voice from the doorway. "Breakfast is served."

Suzy stomped inside, slamming the screen door in Lily's face. Lily felt as if it had hit her—that and maybe a ton of bricks.

By the time she sat down with a plate of runny scrambled eggs in front of her, all Lily could do was push them around with her fork. D. J. reached over and took it out of her hand.

"They're gonna end up on the floor if you keep that up," she said.

"You haven't made up your mind, huh?" Maggie said, in her usual direct way.

Lily shook her head miserably. "It's not that I don't like you guys—I do—but Suzy's been my friend for a long time."

"Can't she make new friends?" D. J. said. "You did."

Lily had to stop and soak that in. *So it's true. They think I'm their friend. I want to be—I so do!*

Genevieve cleared her throat. "I think I know how Lily feels, though," she said. She glanced at Alexandria, who was staring down at the eggs she had smothered in ketchup. "If me and Alex hadn't been in the same cabin and this had been us, I would have trouble deciding too."

Alexandria's head came up. "You would?" she said. "You wouldn't just be with me?"

"Uh, crew?" Jackie said.

They all looked at her. " 'Let's put this discussion on hold until we get to Bible study, okay? I think it could make all of this easier for you."

Lily had never seen a group of twelve-year-olds so anxious to get to a Bible study class — herself included. They all endured the opening songs, impatiently rolling their eyes at each other and plowing down another whole cabin of girls getting to their corner when it was finally time.

"How do you get *that* kind of enthusiasm going?" another counselor asked Jackie.

Lily didn't wait to hear the answer as she slid in between Maggie and D. J. Genevieve and Alexandria sat together as usual, but Alexandria stared straight ahead and blinked as if she were holding back tears. Lily felt an ache for her.

"Matthew 12:46–50," Jackie said.

There were Bibles this time. Pages rustled noisily.

"Is that in the Old Testament or the New Testament?" Maggie whispered to Lily.

"Read it for us, D. J.," Jackie said.

D. J. sat up importantly and read the story of Jesus' mother and brothers showing up and trying to get to him when Jesus was talking to a crowd. When somebody told Jesus they were there and wanted a word with him, he said, "Who is my mother, and who are my brothers?"

"Pointing to his disciples," D. J. read, "he said, 'Here are my mother and my brothers. For whoever does the will of my Father in heaven is my brother and sister and mother.'"

D. J. looked up, puzzled. "I don't get it."

"That's because it's about Lily," Maggie said.

She said it as if it were a proven fact. *This from the girl who didn't know Matthew was in the New Testament?* Lily thought. But she leaned forward and listened.

"Tell us some more," Jackie said.

"Her Girlz are like Jesus' mother and brothers," Maggie said. "Only every girl in this camp is one of the Girlz right now. And especially us — we're like the disciples."

"Does that make Lily Jesus?" Genevieve said.

"No!" Lily said.

"But I think Maggie's on the right track," Jackie said. "Whoever obeys the heavenly Father's will is part of the family. We're here to serve all the members of our family, not just the ones we came with."

"But if I'm not serving Suzy, who *is* gonna take care of her?" Lily said.

"It's not like she's living in a little hut by herself," Maggie said. "She has other girls in her cabin."

"She says they don't like her," Lily said.

"Do you think that's really true?" Jackie asked.

"Maybe. I thought that myself when I first — "

She stopped and looked at the girls who were all looking back at her with such concern in their eyes. It occurred to her at that moment that they really didn't want her to move out of the cabin. The very girls she had thought she could never fit in with here wanted her to be with them.

"Why did you think the girls in the cabin didn't like you, Lily?" Jackie said.

"Because they didn't know me," Lily said.

"We didn't know you because you kept all to yourself," D. J. said. "No offense or anything."

Lily could almost hear a light switching on in her head. "The best way I could help Suzy is to tell her how I finally made friends in my cabin so she can do the same thing. Then *they* can help her get over her homesickness."

Jackie was nodding, but not nearly so enthusiastically as the girls. Lily thought D. J.'s head was going to fly right off her neck.

"So you're staying," Maggie said, once again as if she were stating a scientific fact.

"Yeah," Lily said. "I am."

The cheer that went up made Lily want to cry. Only this time, the tears were happy ones.

But the tears that poured down Suzy's face when Lily broke the news to her at the water fountain during the break were anything but joyful.

"You're not the friend I thought you were, Lily Robbins!" she cried. To Lily's dismay, she even stomped her foot. Her little hands were in balls at her sides.

"I *am* your friend," Lily said, warily watching the fists. "So you have to listen to me — just open yourself up to the girls in your cabin, and they'll help you."

"I don't want them!" Suzy said. "And I don't want you either! Not ever again!"

She turned on her heel and ran, leaving Lily standing at the water fountain listening to the faucet drip. Before she could even sigh, Maggie and Genevieve and D. J. and Alexandria surrounded her.

"It didn't go well," Maggie said, matter-of-factly.

Lily shook her head.

"You did the right thing," D. J. said, slinging her arm around Lily's shoulders.

Genevieve was nodding. "That had to be hard. You were so brave."

"You think so?' Lily said. "You're not just saying that?"

All heads shook — even Jackie's. Lily smiled at them through a shimmer of tears.

"Okay, crew — let's get on with this treasure hunt," Jackie said. "Maggie — you take the map."

Each of the girls — except for Maggie — hugged Lily before she joined Maggie and the map. Jackie hung back with Lily.

"They were so nice to me," Lily whispered to her. "I'm supposed to be serving them — but they're the ones serving me instead."

"I think you'll be surprised," Jackie said. "I think you'll be very surprised."

Chapter 10

The end of the first week of camp arrived before Lily saw it coming. She and the Sisters of the Sea were busy every afternoon, learning the basics of sailing. At first, Lily didn't want to get back in a boat ever again after her keeling-over disaster, but Cherie was patient.

"Sailing doesn't come naturally to everyone," she told Lily as she was buckling her life jacket for her — because Lily was shaking too hard to do it herself. "But you can still learn enough to enjoy it. There will be some part on the crew that you'll play that no one else can. Give yourself a break, eh?"

Jackie assigned Alexandria as Lily's permanent sailing partner. She was definitely less annoying than Maggie, and she had sailed a lot before. That made Lily feel better.

"I know I'm lousy," Lily told her, "so I'm not even going to try to be better than you. Besides, if I get in trouble you'll know what to tell me."

"Atta girl, Lily," Cherie said. "That's the spirit."

But Alexandria didn't seem all that thrilled about it — at least not at first. The first day they sailed together, Lily saw her looking long-ingly at Genevieve as she boarded the *Mermaid* with Jackie and Mag-gie and D. J.

She'd rather be with Genevieve than me, Lily thought. That made her heart start to dive, but she caught it in midsink. *I'm supposed to be serving her—and I so know how she feels.*

So Lily did everything she could to make Alexandria feel at ease. She complimented her on her tan and her sunstreaked hair and how confident she was about tacking and trimming. She bought her a miniature sailboat from the canteen to mark their being sailing part-ners and sent her a Girlz Gram through the camp mail without sign-ing her name. Finally, after a few days, Alexandria stopped watching Genevieve as if she were going to sail off the end of the earth every time she boarded the *Mermaid* with D. J. and Maggie instead of the *Francesca* with her.

There were the other girls to serve too, though figuring out how was hard for Lily. Genevieve and D. J. seemed to have everything they needed. Maggie seemed to need things Lily couldn't imagine how she could provide—like knowing when to stop asking questions. Every night Maggie started in as soon as the lights were out. "Does your Girlz Only Group actually have meetings? Do you, like, use Robert's Rules of Order? Do you elect officers and everything?"

It was a good thing Jackie was providing Lily with quiet time and an alone place every morning so she could talk to God. Sometimes she wrote to him in her journal, but most of the time she just talked. She learned from wishing Maggie would hush up to be quiet herself and let God do some of the talking. He talked, she was sure, by making it more and more fun to participate in everything in the cabin and by easing the ache for home. When she finally got her first letter from Dad, she didn't even feel like crying, although the note from Tessa that he'd tucked inside did give her a temporary throat lump.

Deer Lily,

*Cum home! It is boaring heer wihtout you. Otto is dep-
resed. He bit Joe. Don't forgit me.*

Tessa

Lily read it eleven times and then shared it with the Sisters. Maggie
wanted to know why a nine-year-old couldn't spell better than that,
but the rest of the girls had to pass the Kleenex around.

The only thing God didn't seem to be talking about was how to
deal with Suzy.

Every day at meals, Lily couldn't help searching for Suzy with her
eyes. She would always find her at her cabin table, picking at her food
and shrinking from the conversation going on around her. Suzy's
freckle-faced counselor looked as if she were trying hard to draw her
in, but Suzy was obviously having none of it.

She shouldn't have a college kid, Lily thought. *She should have
somebody wise like Jackie.*

She wanted to hug Suzy hard and talk to her about ways she could
let the other girls get to know her. But whenever Suzy did look up and
catch Lily's eye, the sadness on her face pinched into anger and she
looked away. It was obvious it wasn't going to do any good to try to
touch her.

She'd rip my hand off! Lily thought.

She didn't worry about Reni and Kresha. It didn't hurt anymore to
see them howling and carrying on with their cabin mates, because now
Lily was doing her own howling and carrying on with the Sisters. She
knew that all the way home from camp, she and the Girlz would be
sharing stories in the van, and she was saving hers up.

On Saturday at the end of the first week, the Sisters of the Sea were
set to go to the dining hall after they'd changed clothes from their sail.
Jackie emerged from her little nook with a jacket slung over her shoulder and said, "Sweatshirts or jackets, everybody."

"It's at least 82 degrees in the dining hall," Maggie said. "We'll roast in jackets."

"We aren't going to the dining hall," Jackie said.

"Why?"

"How come?"

"Where *are* we eating?"

Jackie held up her hand. "Surprise," she said. "Follow me."

Maggie, of course, didn't bother to stop asking questions even for a minute as they followed Jackie, giggling all the way down the path toward the bay. Lily ignored her as D. J. looped her arm through Lily's. The anticipation was delicious.

And the real thing was even better.

Waiting for them on the beach was a small fire in a ring of stones and a cooler full of hot dogs and sodas and the makings for S'mores.

"We get to cook hot dogs — right here on the beach?" Genevieve said.

"I knew that," Maggie said. "I mean — it only made sense."

She went on to explain why, but for once it didn't bother Lily. This was *too* good — the sun going down behind them, turning the bay water golden — a fire crackling just for them — four girls she was living with every day all gathered around with their faces flushed from sailing and happiness — the warm way her chest felt, replacing the ache she could barely remember now.

I don't think I've ever been this happy in my whole life, she thought.

And then she got happier. After they'd consumed every hot dog in the cooler and were each on a second S'more, Jackie said, "Do you want to hear about your project?"

"Does a chicken have lips?" D. J. said. "Yes!"

"Wait," Maggie said. "Technically, that would be a no. Chickens don't really have lips."

"Maggie — " Lily took a breath. This felt like serving. She sure hoped it was. "Now would be a really good time for you to pay attention to your own lips," she said, "and close them — okay?"

Maggie shrugged happily. D. J. gave Lily a grateful look, and Lily knew she'd just saved Maggie from a D. J. chewing out.

"Tell us about the project, Jackie," Genevieve said. "I'm dying right now!"

Although Maggie muttered that Genevieve wasn't really dying, she kept quiet as Jackie explained.

"I'd rather call it a pilgrimage instead of a project," she said. "Next Thursday, we are going to sail out to South Deer Island, set up camp, and spend the night. Then we'll sail back the next day." She grinned at the girls. "Does that sound like something you'd like to do?"

"Are you kidding?" D. J. said. She actually got up and did a dance in the sand.

The rest of the girls — even Maggie — shrieked at top pitch.

"I'm going to take that as a yes," Jackie said. She was beaming at them like a mom. Lily loved her at that moment.

"Nate and Cherie are going with us," Jackie said. "But you'll work as a team to get everything done. There are some things you'll do together, such as pitch the tents and clean up after meals. But each of you will have an individual job as well."

"Like what?" Maggie said. She obviously couldn't hold back any longer.

"I have a list," Jackie said. "Why don't you take a look at it?"

Lily crowded in with the rest of them and craned to get a good view. It was one time when it paid to be tall.

The list sizzled before her eyes, and she knew immediately it was going to be hard to pick just one thing.

Lead devotions. That was *so* right down her alley. She could imagine herself on the beach, firelight on her face, sharing what she was learning about God while the water lapped against the dock in the background — aah!

But then there was *Double-check all packing; ensure that we have everything we need.* That, Lily decided, was such a perfect job for her it was practically screaming her name. It would give her a chance to use her leadership skills — she'd get to carry a clipboard around and have a pencil tucked behind her ear as she gently questioned Maggie about the missing sleeping bag or the box of matches they couldn't live without.

She was itching for the pencil in question so she could put her name next to that one, when Jackie said, "I'd like for each of you to think about all the things you've learned about yourselves this week through our studies and activities and your quiet times with God and *then* pick a job."

Lily glanced up to see Jackie looking right at her.

Oh, Lily thought. *I bet I know what she's thinking. This is my chance to serve all the girls.* She sagged a little. *I did promise, after all, and so far they've been doing most of the serving.*

Stifling a sigh, Lily looked at the list again. The job that almost waved its little hand and said, "Pick me — pick me!" was all *about* serving: Plan meals and prepare for cooking.

It sounded so boring, nobody else was going to want it, she was sure of that. *That would be serving,* she thought. *Letting everybody else have what they want.*

"I've got mine picked out," she said — quickly, so she wouldn't change her mind.

Without so much as a blink, Jackie handed her a pencil. Lily put her initials next to "planning meals."

"You want *that* one?" Maggie said.

"Lily can choose any one she wants," Jackie said. There was a smile in her voice. "Unless, of course, somebody else has a mad desire to do it."

"Not me!" Maggie said. "I'm taking 'fire starter.'" She looked around hopefully but nobody else jumped on it.

D. J. chose "double-checker," and Genevieve picked "devotions leader," and Alexandria seemed happy with "tent supervision." Each one of them asked Lily if she was sure she didn't want that one. Lily just kept shaking her head.

"We're gonna be an awesome team, Sisters," D. J. said.

"This'll be the best pilgrimage we ever went on," Genevieve said.

"It probably will, since none of us has ever been on one before," Maggie said.

"Maggie," Lily said.

"What?" Maggie said.

"Hush *up!*" they all said.

Maggie grinned as if they'd just elected her cabin president.

They stayed on the beach until the fire dwindled and all the graham crackers and Hershey bars were gone. Then they walked back to the cabin five abreast, whispering as if talking out loud would mean the magical night was over.

But the magic continued in the days that followed.

In Bible study every morning, they read all the stories of Jesus going on boat trips with his disciples. It made Lily feel so inspired that she burst out one day, "I wish Jesus were going to be there with us!"

"He will be," Jackie said. "He definitely will be."

"You mean just in spirit, right?" Maggie said. "You're not talking about the Second Coming?"

"I can't predict *that,*" Jackie said, eyes twinkling. "But having him there in spirit isn't any small thing."

"This is gonna be special," Genevieve said. "You just wait for devotions."

For one jealous moment, Lily wished she were the one planning them. She was great with imagination—she'd have them seeing Jesus on the beach.

But the excitement in Genevieve's eyes was something Lily didn't want to take away. Besides, this was a whole new Genevieve to her. She was so far from the selfish, shallow, popular girl Lily had first thought she was. Lily couldn't even conjure up that image anymore.

Besides, Lily's job was turning out to be more fun than it had looked like on paper.

First she got to sit down and plan the meals any way she wanted to — and her "culinary imagination," as Maggie called it, ran wild. When it came time to show it to the kitchen staff for approval, Lily got a little nervous and changed T-bone steaks to hamburgers and ham and cheese omelettes to pancakes, and even then she was afraid the cook would say it was too much. But the cook nodded as she read Lily's menus, and she tapped the erased parts with a flour-covered finger.

"Why don't you have steaks?" she said. "They're actually easier to deal with on a trip like this, and you don't have to take so many condiments — you know, ketchup, mustard."

"I really wanted to do fish and loaves of bread," Lily said. "You know, like the miracle? But I guess that's too complicated."

Cook rubbed her nose with her finger, covering it with flour as well. Then she said, "I don't see why you couldn't do that. How about for breakfast — then you would also be reminding them of the breakfast Jesus cooked for the disciples after the Resurrection."

"Oh, yeah!" Lily said. "But what if everybody doesn't like fish — and how would we do that?"

"I can help you," Cook said. She grinned a floury grin at Lily. "That's why they pay me the big bucks."

Lily loved working with Cook, especially when it was time to put together what she called a mess kit.

"It's not a very nice name for something to do with food," Lily said as she was compiling the necessary pans and utensils. "Especially for a pilgrimage."

"It's very nautical," Cook told her. "On a ship, the captain's dining room is called the Captain's Mess."

"Yuck!" Lily said.

"Now, the place you'll be storing the food on the boat is called the cuddy," Cook said. She winked. "You can impress everybody with that."

Lily made a note of it.

By Tuesday she had all the basics covered, and it was time for the fun part. She hadn't known there would *be* a fun part until Cook told her she could come up with a theme and choose her paper plates and napkins and things like that to match it. Lily filled up two pages in her journal with ideas before she settled on The Miracles as her theme.

Then it was a matter of finding small enough baskets and jars to fit in the cuddy, not to mention coming up with paper plate ideas. When she presented it all to the Sisters of the Sea, however, they loved it so much that when Alexandria said she wasn't sure she liked salmon on her bagels, D. J. said, "If Lily picked it, I bet it's gonna be delicious."

Lily later told Alexandria that her feelings wouldn't be hurt if she had her bagel without salmon. This serving thing was getting easier all the time.

On Wednesday, the day before the trip, Lily got to go into town with all the food people from the other cabins to buy the supplies that weren't available in the kitchen. Lily squealed when she saw Reni waiting to get in the van.

"Lil!" Reni squealed back.

They ran to each other and hugged themselves around in a circle. They saw each other every day at meals and activities, when they waved to each other and yelled things back and forth. But D. J. had been right that first day when she'd said they'd be so busy with cabin stuff, they wouldn't have much time to hang out with other people. It felt so good to be hugging Reni.

99

They sat next to each other in the Camp Galilee van and chattered the whole way there, the whole way back, and the entire time they were in the general store. Reni helped Lily find colored paper plates she could draw miracle symbols on, and Lily advised Reni on nutrition bars to go in backpacks for her cabin's big climb. One of the subjects that came up as they talked, of course, was Suzy.

"She's so bummed out, I can hardly get her to say more than two words to me when I see her," Reni said.

"At least you get two words," Lily said. "She won't talk to me at all. She won't even look at me." Lily sighed. "I think she hates me."

"That's what she says."

Lily's eyes widened.

"She doesn't really mean it," Reni said quickly. "She just says it because she's mad at you."

"Oh, thanks," Lily said. "That really helps." She slanted a glance at Reni as they walked to the van with their packages. "Do you think I did the right thing, not moving to her cabin after Zooey left?"

Reni squinted at her through the sun. "She actually asked you to do that?"

Lily nodded.

"That was *so* not fair for her to even ask you that, Lily!" Reni said. "So don't feel bad for one second." She shook her head. "The reason she did that is because you always do everything for all of us."

"I do?" Lily said.

"Yeah — all the time. I hated it that you weren't in my cabin at first. I still think it would've been a total blast if you had been. But then I wouldn't of done stuff for myself, like get to know people — keep track of my toothbrush — all that." She stopped beside the van, shifted her packages to her other hip, and looked soberly at Lily. "You'll always be my best friend in the whole world, Lil, but I made some friends here that I'm gonna write to and stuff. It feels kinda good to know other people like me too."

"Yeah," Lily said. "I know what you mean."

"And when we get home, I'm not gonna let you do everything for me anymore, and neither is Kresha. We talked about it, and we decided we have to stand on our own two feet."

Reni climbed into the van, and Lily stood, staring.

What is she talking about? she thought. *I thought I came here to learn how to serve. Was I already doing it?*

What was even more confusing was how she was going to continue serving at home when her friends didn't need her to. And how was she supposed to stop serving them when she didn't even know she was doing it in the first place?

She was going to have a major topic for God *that* night, she decided.

Lily and Reni continued to chatter on the way back to camp, and Lily felt just a small pang of her old homesickness when they had to give each other a final hug and go back to their own cabins. They were just letting go of each other when Mary Francis appeared on the driveway, lifting her head as if she were looking for someone. She had a phone in her hand.

"Lily?" she said. "Is Lily Robbins here?"

"That's you, Lil!" Reni said. She waved her arm at Mary Francis, who hurried over with the phone.

"There you are," she said. She handed Lily the phone. "It's for you—it's your father."

All Lily could think of as she took the phone from Mary Francis was that something was wrong.

Her voice shook. "Hello?"

Chapter 11

"Is that you, Lilliputian?" Dad said.

"Daddy—what's wrong?" Lily said. "Is it Tessa? It's Tessa, isn't it? What happened?"

She could hear her father chuckling softly, and it made her want to clench her teeth. How could he laugh at a time like this?

"Slow down, now," he said. "Nothing's wrong. Can't a father call up his daughter who he hasn't seen in almost two weeks and see how she's doing?"

"He can," Lily said slowly. "But he doesn't—usually. Especially when we're not allowed to get phone calls from our parents."

"This is a special case. I begged."

"No, you did not!"

"I did. I told Johnnie that your letters just didn't sound like you—"

"Who's Johnnie?" Lily said.

"Your counselor. Isn't that her name?"

"Jackie!" Lily started to giggle. Okay, maybe everything *was* normal after all.

"She said you were struggling," Dad said, "so I had to talk to you. I went to the top, and Mary Katherine finally gave in."

Lily didn't correct him this time. She just laughed. "I'm not struggling anymore," she said. "I love it here, and I have all these new friends."

"Excellent." She could hear the grin in his voice. "Are you running the camp yet, or do you need another week for that?"

"Oh, no! I'm never going to do that. That isn't my real gift, Dad. I've learned that."

There was a long pause. Then she could hear him grinning again. "Maybe we should have signed you up for the whole summer then!"

By the time they said good-bye, Dad sounded reassured that Lily was no longer struggling.

"Please tell Tessa that I'm not forgetting her," Lily said. "Tell her I think about her all the time."

"And vice versa. We hear nothing but 'Wait 'til Lily sees me do this.' She's almost walking on her own."

Again Lily felt the pang. But as she hung up, it softened to a warm place in her chest. She was glad she had them all at home — Dad and Mom and Joe and Art and Tessa and Otto. But she was glad to be here too. It felt rich, like a thick chocolate sauce. She grinned to herself. She was spending *way* too much time thinking about food lately.

Although the week was speeding by, the last few hours before the trip seemed to crawl. Even Maggie, little Miss Matter-of-Fact, was so restless that she reopened her bag five times to make sure she had enough matches and that the fire extinguisher was still in there.

"You're doing my job," D. J. told her. "I won't need to double check any of your stuff!"

"Every minute is the same length as any other minute," Maggie said to Lily. "Why do these seem longer?"

Lily decided it was good to see Maggie starting to act like a kid instead of a professor.

Finally, after a lunch in the dining hall that everybody was too excited to eat, they picked up their bundles and headed for the bay. Cook took off her apron long enough to help Lily carry the coolers down and then stood there watching proudly while Lily placed everything carefully in the cuddy.

"This one is great with food," Cook told Cherie.

"This must be that one thing I can do on the crew that nobody else can do," Lily said. "Remember when you told me that?"

"Yeah," Cherie said, "but I don't think this is it."

"It sure isn't sailing!" Lily said as she waved good-bye to Cook and watched her bustle off down the dock.

"Sure it is. In fact, I have something to tell you."

Cherie sat on one of the benches and motioned for Lily to do the same.

"Nate is taking a lot of the supplies on the big sloop, and he planned to just sail alone," she said, "but the wind is pretty brisk today, and he wants a crew. We thought Alexandria would be best since she has the most sailing experience."

"Who's gonna sail with us?" Lily said. She bit her tongue to keep from adding, "Not Maggie." She was tolerating Maggie better these days, but she was still like a mosquito that asked questions.

"Nobody," Cherie said. "Just you and me."

"But I can't be the whole crew!" Lily said. "I'm not good enough!"

"Sure ya are." Cherie leaned forward and put both hands on Lily's knees. "No, you aren't the pick-it-right-up sailor like Maggie, and that's because you don't have her scientific math mind. There's a lot about sailing that's just physics. But ever since that second day, when you keeled over, you've stopped trying to be impressive. You haven't been going after being the best sailor in the history of boating—you've just been concentrating on learning what you can." Cherie wrinkled her zinc-oxide nose as she smiled. "You've learned more than you think you have. You're turning out to be a pretty decent sailor."

"You really think we can sail, just you and me, all the way to the island?"

"Cherie could probably sail it by herself," said a voice from the dock above them.

Cherie looked up at Maggie and lowered her sunglasses on her nose. "Don't you have something you need to be doing?" she said.

"No, I have all my stuff done — "

"Go!"

Maggie skittered off, and Cherie turned to Lily, pushing her glasses back into place. "I'm sorry she said that."

But Lily shook her head and grinned. "To tell you the truth, it made me feel better. If I do mess up, it doesn't mean we'll automatically keel over and drown."

Cherie threw her head back and laughed. "You are something else, Lily. What do you say we get under way?"

And so all three of the boats made their way out into the bay. Lily's heart pounded while she cleated the halyard to the mast, checked to make sure that all of the lines attached to the mainsail were free to run, and pulled the mainsail to the top of the mast. As she cleated the end of the halyard in place, she glanced up to discover Cherie grinning at her.

"You did great," she said. "Now let's trim her in."

Lily was surprised to discover that she *did* know what to do. She even helped Cherie raise the headsail after that and hauled in one of the sheets, a job Alexandria had always done before.

"Look at us!" Cherie called out. "We are fully under sail!"

There was time for one high-five and one look out on the bay at the other two boats before they lowered the centerboard. Sails billowed. All the boats leaned gracefully. D. J.'s laughter floated out on the wind. It was a scene Lily wanted to remember always — even the crackly sound of Maggie talking. For once, it made Lily smile.

In fact, everything made her smile. Cherie calling out, "Pull the traveler up to the windward side," and Lily knowing what that meant. Water splashing and sparkling as they parted it with their bow. Salt on her lips. The wind suddenly shifting, sending Cherie and herself scurrying to trim.

"I'm sailing!" Lily cried out once.

The boat leaned then, and Lily let out a shriek as her elbow grazed the cats paws on the water.

"Ready about!" Cherie called.

Lily held her breath. It was time to tack.

Fingers shaking again, she uncleated the leeward headsail and kept it on the winch, ready to free.

"Ready!" Lily said.

Cherie nodded. "Coming about!"

Lily did her part — she cast off the leeward sheet, hauled in a new leeward sheet until it was tight, and wrapped it two more times around the winch. This time, it didn't come loose. There was no keeling. No sails dipping into the water.

As the boat tilted playfully to the starboard, Cherie gave Lily a thumbs-up. Lily laughed and shouted, "I want to do that again!"

Yet when they sailed into a tiny inlet on the island behind Nate and Alexandria and let the anchor down just close enough to the dock so that they could swing out onto the steps, Lily was ready for a rest. After she and Cherie shook out the sails and furled them neatly and coiled and hung up the sheets, she could let the concentration fall away. It felt so free.

When all the supplies had been carried up to the beach and the Sisters had put up their big tent — with Alexandria giving instructions — and gathered kindling and wood for the fire — under Maggie's detailed direction — Jackie said they could relax and go for a swim.

Splashing and squealing and riding on the shoulders of a slippery friend had never, ever been so much fun for Lily. The cold water made her teeth chatter, and everyone's lips turned blue up to their noses, but no one cared. It was pure bliss.

When they were practically numb, they all stumbled up to the beach, where Maggie's fire was crackling and spitting around potatoes wrapped in foil and Nate was cooking the steaks on a tiny grill. Lily threw on sweats over her swimsuit and set her Miracles table on two spread-out blankets. Out came the red and yellow and blue paper plates with fish and crosses and lambs carefully drawn on them — and the matching napkins, which she had folded neatly into fish, origami style.

"I never ate in a restaurant this beautiful," Genevieve said when they'd gathered and blessed the food.

"And I betcha you never had a view like that either, eh?" Cherie said. She pointed out over the water, which was violet in the dusk. The moon shook out silvery flakes on the tiny pointed waves, to match the stars above them.

"I told you God would be here," Jackie said.

But they hadn't seen anything yet. When supper was cleaned up, the Sisters of the Sea gathered around Maggie's fire — which looked like something on the cover of a camping magazine — and Genevieve began her devotion.

"Lily gave me the idea for this," she said, "only she doesn't even know it."

She read them the story of the loaves and fishes provided by a little boy, which Jesus blessed and miraculously used to feed thousands.

"Jesus will perform miracles for us if we let him," Genevieve said. "We just have to be like that little boy and give him all that we have. That's when miracles happen." She took a big breath. Leading a devotion, Lily saw, was hard work. "So now I want you guys to all think whether you have given everything you have these two weeks. Think and pray really hard. A miracle — maybe a tiny one — will happen in your life."

"You know this for a fact?" Maggie said.

Lily heard Alexandria sigh. D. J. turned and gave Maggie a hard look.

"Is this really the time for one of your questions?" she said.

"I'm serious," Maggie said.

Her voice sounded thick. It was then that Lily saw the tears sparkling behind her glasses.

"I want to believe in things like miracles," she said. "But I've been taught that if you can't prove something, you know, with facts or numbers, it isn't true and you shouldn't trust it."

"You can't prove that a miracle is a miracle," Jackie said. "You just know it. Aren't there things that you know but you can't prove?"

"I'd have to think about it," Maggie said.

"Then do it. That's your assignment. See if you can give us an answer before we leave. That's day after tomorrow."

"No!" D. J. wailed. "It can't be that soon!"

"A real miracle would be if we got back to camp tomorrow and they'd extended it the rest of the summer," Genevieve said.

Jackie looked at Lily. "What do you think about that, Lily?"

"That would be a great miracle," Lily said. "I could get into that."

Jackie gave her a huge grin.

The Sisters had big plans for what they were going to do in their tent that night, most of which involved scary stories and hair makeovers. But eyes seemed to slam shut the minute bodies crept into sleeping bags. Within minutes, Lily was the only one awake.

It was perfect for some alone time with God, and Lily closed her eyes and let herself listen to God the way she'd learned to do over the past ten days. But she was restless like she sometimes got when she knew she hadn't gotten all her homework done.

She wriggled around in her sleeping bag until Maggie started to stir. Lily waited until she settled down again and then crept out of the tent and curled up next to what was left of the fire. In a few minutes, she felt a blanket being draped over her shoulders, and Jackie sat down beside her.

"I could hear your wheels turning all the way from my tent," Jackie said. "Do you need to be alone with God, or do you want to talk?"

"I think I want to talk," Lily said. "'Cause I'm not exactly hearing God right now."

"Shoot." Jackie poked at the fire. The flames startled from their sleep and licked at the air. "From the look on your face, I think we're going to be here a while," she said.

Lily took a deep breath. "Okay — I think I've done almost my whole assignment you gave me."

"I think you've done all of it," Jackie said. "What have you missed?"

"I haven't served every girl. Every time I try, they end up serving me. I hope being the food person counts."

"It certainly counts," Jackie said, "but I think you've served them individually as well." She held up two fingers. "You've definitely served Genevieve and Alexandria by showing them that they can be okay without being attached at the hip and that it's good to make other friends. They were watching you during that whole Suzy thing. Your decision made a huge difference to them — and then you made Alexandria feel at ease with you so she wasn't so focused on Genevieve. Alex was the one I was worried about, and she's doing fine, thanks to you."

"I didn't know I was doing all that, though, so I don't think that's really serving."

"I think it's the best kind of serving. Look at Maggie."

Lily groaned. "I'm barely nice to her."

"She's hard to be nice to — but you've done it because you're a good person. Even if you were gritting your teeth, you still made her feel like she was part of things. There have been times when she has forgotten her career goals and actually acted like a kid. You couldn't do anything better for her."

"What about D. J.?" Lily said.

Jackie poked at the fire some more. "She's your special friend in the cabin."

"I want to serve her *really*, though."

Jackie grinned. "When you take on an assignment, you don't fool around, do you?"

"Unh-uh."

"Then I say pray about it and watch. Your opportunity will come. D. J. doesn't have everything she needs." She patted Lily's shoulder. "Besides, just by following the spiritual disciplines I gave you, you've served people in ways you weren't even aware of. Maybe only God will ever know how much you've helped D. J."

Lily nodded — and yawned. She suddenly felt so peaceful that she was sure she could sleep right there on the ground. Jackie helped her to the tent, where she was barely inside her sleeping bag before she was asleep.

The salmon and bagels made the perfect miracle breakfast the next day, and the swim and the hunt for seashells and the sail back to camp were like mini-miracles themselves. It all unfurled the way the sails did in the wind, carrying them forward like silken wings.

But they also carried the girls to their last few hours at camp. Almost before they could exchange addresses and promises to write weekly for the rest of their lives, the Sisters of the Sea were sitting in their cabin, duffel bags packed and faces long. There was nothing to do now but wait for rides and feel sad.

Lily was just considering bursting into tears when Reni poked her head in.

"I gotta talk to you, Lil," she said.

"We can talk in here," Lily said.

"Yeah, we're the Girlz too," Maggie said.

Reni gave Maggie a doubtful look, but Lily nodded. Even if it wasn't quite true, it was okay that Maggie thought it was. Like Jackie said, she needed to feel like she belonged.

"I just talked to Suzy," Reni said as she joined Lily on her bed. "This ride home isn't gonna be that much fun."

"Does she still hate me?" Lily said.

"She didn't say that, but she told me that she called her parents yesterday and asked them to come pick her up so she wouldn't have to ride with you."

"Rude!" Genevieve said.

"Are they coming?" Lily said.

"No. They said she has to ride with your dad." Reni held out both palms, as if she were out of answers. "I say we just try to pretend nothing happened and maybe she'll snap out of it."

"That sounds hard," D. J. said. "I don't think I could do that."

"Me either," Lily said.

"Sounds like you need a miracle."

They all looked at Maggie, who looked back at them as if she'd merely suggested they needed popcorn.

"You believe in them, don't you?" she said.

Lily nodded.

"So pray for one."

"Yeah, but you have to give all you have too," Genevieve said. She was up on her knees on her bed, eyes intrigued.

"Lily's given just about everything she could," Alexandria said. "I don't see what else she could do."

"There's gotta be something," Lily said. She felt a little better. At least she had something to focus on.

She looked then at D. J., who had her nose pressed to the screen, watching for her parents to come down the path. *I still haven't figured out a way to serve her,* Lily thought. *It is gonna take a miracle for me to think of something for her and for Suzy in the next fifteen minutes!*

"Oh, no," D. J. said.

She pulled away from the window and slumped down on the bed like a deflating beach toy.

"What's wrong?" Genevieve asked.

D. J. flung a hand toward the window. "They brought her."

"Who?" Lily said. "Your sister?"

"Yes. Here I am feeling all good about myself, and now I'm gonna lose that before I even get to the car."

"Wow," Maggie said from the window. "She really *is* pretty."

"Maggie, hush up," Genevieve said.

But it was too late. D. J. deflated completely. She was getting tears in her eyes.

"Okay, wait a minute," Lily said. "We're not gonna forget everything we learned here before we even leave the cabin!"

"What did I learn?" D. J. said.

Lily climbed over Reni to sit beside D. J. "If I can learn that I don't have to be the best at absolutely everything, then you can learn that the Amazing Valerie out there isn't either."

"She better hurry up, then," Maggie said, "because they're coming this way."

Lily took D. J. by the shoulders. "You are the *best* at keeping everybody cheered up. You say something funny about every ten minutes."

"You're the best at keeping everything organized," Genevieve said. "I would have forgotten half my stuff for our pilgrimage thing if it hadn't been for you."

"You're the best at telling me when I'm talking too much," Maggie said. She grinned. "I bet everybody appreciated that."

D. J.'s olive face was tinged in pink. "You guys aren't just saying this stuff to make me feel better?"

"Nah," Maggie said. "I don't even know how to do that."

Lily waited for D. J.'s wonderful grin, but to her dismay, she burst into tears. The Sisters looked at each other helplessly.

"I want to take you guys home with me," D. J. said into the hands that covered her face.

"You can!" Lily said. "We're all inside each other now."

"Yeah, even I believe that," Maggie said.

D. J. shook her head. "It's not the same."

"No," Lily said. "It's a God thing — so it's even better."

"They're here," Maggie whispered loudly.

They all looked at D. J. and held their breaths. Slowly she seemed to inflate again. Smacking the tears off of her face, she stood up, grabbed her duffel bag and her backpack, and squared her shoulders.

"I can do this," she said.

"'Course you can," Lily said.

"We love you, D. J.!" Alexandria and Genevieve said together.

As D. J. marched out the door, they all gathered at the window to watch her reunion with her family, noses pressed to the screen the way D. J. herself always did.

"I don't get it," Maggie said. "D. J.'s just as pretty as her sister — maybe prettier."

For once, Maggie is absolutely right, Lily thought. She had the feeling that she'd just served D. J. — in a big way.

Now the only one left was Suzy.

Genevieve and Alexandria took off next, amid tearful good-byes, and Reni went back to her cabin to get her bags. Jackie walked with Maggie and Lily to the main building to wait for their rides. A very tall man with a beard waved to Maggie, although there wasn't a trace of a smile anywhere on him.

"Is that your dad?" Lily said.

Maggie nodded. It was the first time in the two weeks Lily had known her that she didn't answer a question with a two-hundred-word paragraph. Lily looked at her closely.

Maggie's shoulders pulled slightly forward until a little bump appeared at the back of her neck. She looked like a timid little bird.

113

"Are you scared of him?" Lily whispered to her.

"Not scared," Maggie whispered back. "I just know he's going to get in my face because I didn't write enough letters or I can't name every single part of a sailboat or something." She looked at Jackie. "Some things you just know, even if you can't prove them. I guess I finished my assignment, huh?"

Jackie shook her head. "This is what you know, Maggie, way down inside you."

Jackie looked at Lily, and for a second Lily had no idea what she was supposed to do. But as she watched Maggie glance nervously at her waiting father and then look back at Lily with longing in her eyes, Lily knew.

She held out her arms and curled them around Maggie. Maggie held on so tight, Lily could barely breathe.

"I get it," Maggie said in that thick voice. And then she walked toward her father with her duffel bag slung over her shoulder. One red sock peeked out through the zipper.

"She's a different Maggie from the one who arrived here two weeks ago," Jackie said. To Lily's surprise, Jackie's voice was thick too.

"Lee-Lee!" somebody called out from behind them.

It was Kresha, of course, running down the path toward her, bags askew and more than one sock poking out of each one. Lily laughed out loud.

"I missed you!" Kresha said, throwing her arms, bags and all, around Lily's neck. A duffel punched against Lily's ear.

"So these are your Girlz," Jackie said, smiling at Reni and Kresha—and Suzy.

"All of them but Zooey," Lily said.

Reni nodded. "I hate leaving here, but I'll be glad to see her."

"I be glad to see us all," Kresha said. "We been so apart." She looked at Suzy. "Right, Suzy?"

Suzy didn't answer. She just shaded her eyes toward the road and said, "Here comes Dr. Robbins."

Lily hugged Jackie as the other Girlz ran toward the van. "Tell me what to do about Suzy!" Lily said into her neck.

"Do what you've been doing," Jackie said. "Serve her."

Lily nodded, though she still didn't have a clue. She felt heavy as she went to Dad and hugged him and turned over her bags.

"You that sad to leave?" Dad said.

"Sort of," Lily said.

He surveyed her with his eyes. "I knew you would be changed," he said. "I'm not disappointed."

Lily turned to climb into the front seat, but Reni was already in it.

"Beat you to it," Reni said. She showed her dimples and pointed behind her.

Lily went to get into the far rear seat, but Kresha was sitting there, grinning at her. The only place left was in the second seat, next to Suzy, who had pulled herself as close to the window as she could and was staring out of it.

Lily glared at Reni, who was all wide-eyed innocence. Lily didn't buy it, but she got into the second seat anyway.

Serve her, Jackie had said.

As Dad pulled the van out onto the main road, Lily's leg hit a grocery bag on the floor, and she peered into it. It was stuffed with crackers, cookies, and enough grapes and bananas to feed an entire zoo. Good ol' Mom.

Lily snatched up a box of Better Cheddars and held it out to Suzy.

"Cracker, honey?" she said.

Suzy shook her head.

"Cookie?"

"No."

"Rice Krispies treats?"

"No — thank you."

"How about a — "

"I don't want anything from you, Lily!"

The air froze inside the van. Lily could see her father's eyes darting toward her in the rearview mirror.

"I'm just trying to serve you — like I learned at camp," Lily said.

Suzy folded her arms across her chest. "If you really wanted to do that, you would have come to be with me when Zooey left."

"Oh, for Pete's sake, Suzy!" Reni jerked herself around in the front seat to face them. "Look — I learned something at camp too. It isn't up to other people to make everything all wonderful for you, the way Lily always does. I had to make other friends — we all did. That's why we were there. We aren't gonna always be together our whole entire lives."

Suzy looked stricken, as if that had never occurred to her before.

"It's true," Lily said. "I'm going away to England in August for a whole year. I thought I wasn't gonna be able to stand it without you all, but now I know I can."

"So you're just going to forget about us, the way you forgot about me at camp," Suzy said.

In the back seat, Kresha said something in Croatian and slapped her own forehead. "Nobody forget about you, Su-zee!" she said. "You are so silly right now!"

Reni grinned. "She picked up that 'right now' thing from the girls in our cabin. She says it all the time."

Suzy was shaking her head, strings of her dark hair sticking to the tears on her cheeks. "The girls in my cabin didn't like me."

"I thought that too, about mine," Lily said. "But then I started acting like I liked them, and things got better."

Kresha gave Suzy a gentle poke on the shoulder. "You start liking us right now — things get better. You'll see."

Lily struggled for something else to say, but it seemed as if they'd pretty much said it all. Now they could only wait for Suzy. As Lily watched the thoughts twist and flinch on Suzy's face, she had a few of her own.

I thought I was going to have to work out this whole thing with Suzy by myself—but Reni and Kresha just sort of jumped in there. I guess that's the way it is with real friends. It's a God thing. I sure hope I find that in England.

"Are you going to be mad at me the whole rest of the summer?" Suzy said, to the ceiling.

"I'm not mad at you now!" Lily said.

"You the one mad right now," Kresha said.

But Suzy shook her head. "I'm not mad. I'm just scared that if I don't have you guys, I'll be all alone like I was at camp!"

"We can *so* work on that," Reni said. She waved it off as if it were a matter of a few minor adjustments in Suzy's brain.

"I love you, Su-zee!" Kresha cried, and then threw her arms around Suzy's neck from behind. They both shrieked so loud, Dad almost went off the road.

Lily just sat back in her seat, Better Cheddars in hand, and smiled to herself. She was sure she could feel God right there in the car.

In fact, she was sure now that she felt God everywhere—even when she didn't have Otto curled up beside her and China to lean on. That, she decided, was a miracle.

She would have to write and tell Maggie.

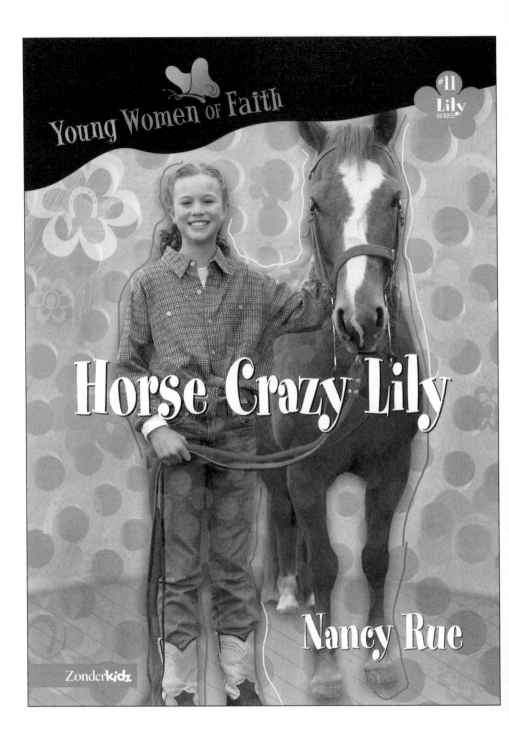

Young Women of Faith

#11
Lily
SERIES

Horse Crazy Lily

Nancy Rue

Zonderkidz

Chapter 1

"Hey, Lily — you comin' or what?"

Lily Robbins glared into the mirror she was standing in front of. She was looking at her own redheaded self, but the glare was intended for her seventeen-year-old brother, Art. He was two floors down and probably tossing his keys from one hand to the other.

"Like he has so much to do on a Saturday afternoon," Lily said to the mirror.

But he *had* agreed to drive her out to Suzy's birthday party.

With a sigh, she untangled her way-long-for-a-twelve-year-old legs and got to the door, where she poked her curly head out and yelled back, "Don't have a cow! I'll be right down."

"Define 'right down,'" Art yelled back.

"Two minutes."

"I'm pulling out of the driveway in exactly two minutes."

Lily scrambled to the closet and dragged out the boots she'd cleaned up for Suzy's party. They brought on a grin. What a great idea Suzy had come up with for her birthday — an afternoon of horseback riding for her and all the Girlz — Lily, Zooey, Reni, and

Kresha. Lily had never been on a horse, though she'd always thought it sounded way cool. She felt like this was as much a present for her as for Suzy.

Lily glanced at her watch and then whipped her mane of curls around, looking for the gift she'd taken a half hour to wrap. She had put it right on the bed — and it should be easy to spot.

Since she'd moved into her new room up here in the attic a week ago, she hadn't had a chance to decorate — what her mother referred to as "cluttering up the place." The only things currently cluttering it were her stuffed animals. She could barely function without them, especially the giant panda, China, who she leaned against during her talking-to-God time every night — with Otto by her side, of course.

"Otto!" Lily said.

She heard him grunt from under the bed, and she dove for it.

"Tell me you don't have Suzy's present!" she said as she lifted up the dust ruffle.

Otto, her little gray mutt, blinked at her through the darkness.

"You do — you are so evil!"

Lily made a snatch for the blue-covered package and managed to get hold of the ribbon. While Otto tugged one way, she yanked the other and pulled dog and gift out into daylight. Otto's scruffy top hair stood up on end.

"I'm lee-ving — " Art called from below.

"Don't! I'm coming!" Lily cried. Grabbing onto the gift — and dangling Otto in midair in the process — she grabbed her denim jacket with her free hand and tore down both flights of stairs. Otto growled and snarled the whole way, but he didn't loosen his little jaws of steel, in spite of Lily's steady stream of "Drop it, you little demon seed! I spent my whole last week's allowance on that!"

Art, arms folded, was waiting at the bottom of the stairs.

"Grab him, Art," Lily said. "Make him let go."

"You gotta be kidding," Art said. He took a step backward. "I'm not touching that dog. He'll bite my hand off."

"What in the world — " Mom said. She appeared out of the dining room, dust rag in one hand, can of furniture polish in the other. Her mouth twitched — in that way it did instead of going into a whole smile. "Otto," she said in her crisp coach's voice. "Drop it."

Otto, of course, didn't — at least not until Mom sprayed some polish into the air above her head. Otto let go of the present and, tucking his tail between his scrawny legs, disappeared up the stairs. He didn't like spray cans.

"Can we go now?" Art said.

"Have fun," Mom said. "And, Lil — don't make any plans to spend the night with anybody tonight. You know tomorrow is a big day."

Lily nodded as she ran toward Art's Subaru — nicknamed Ruby Sue. She managed to slide in before Art got it into gear.

"It's that place over in Columbus, right?" Art said.

"Uh-huh."

"Could she have picked a place farther away?"

"It's the only riding stables in South Jersey, I think," Lily said.

"Tha-at's an exaggeration." Art had picked up a new habit of dragging out his words in a bored voice. Lily thought it must be some cool thing musicians did.

"So — what do you think this Tessa chick is going to be like?" he said with a snicker. "Her mother must have really had it in for her to give her a name like Tessa. What's thaaat about?"

Lily rolled her eyes in his direction. "Her mother probably *did* have it in for her, or she wouldn't have been in all those foster homes. And we're not supposed to talk about all the stuff that's happened to her unless she brings it up, remember?" "Like I'm going to forget. We heard it about a dozen times."

Lily had to agree — he was right about that. Ever since Mom and Dad had found out that the adoption agency had a child for them, they'd been holding family meetings to talk about Tessa, who was about to become their nine-year-old sister.

"She's had a rough time," Dad had explained. "She hasn't had any of the things you kids have had, including love or security or a family."

Mom was a little more direct: "You can't be doing your brother-and-sister routine while she's getting adjusted. No teasing — no kicking under the table — am I clear?"

"Have you noticed how different they are lately when they talk about her?" Art said now. "Now that they've actually met her?"

"No," Lily said. "Well — I did notice that Mom's cleaning the entire house with a toothbrush to get ready for her. You think Tessa's a neat freak?"

Art shook his head. "I saw a list of child psychologists on Dad's desk."

"Don't they send, like, mental patients to them?"

"Nah — half the kids I know are in therapy," Art said. "Whatever the chick's got going on, it's probably not that big a deal. I think Mom and Dad are freakin' a little."

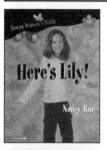

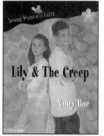

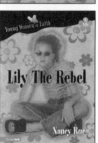

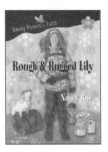
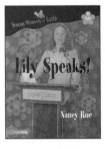

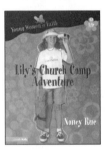
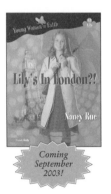
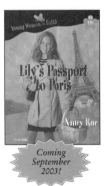

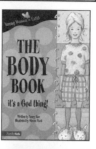

Young Women OF Faith

The Year 'Round Holiday Book
... It's a God Thing!
Softcover 0-310-70256-9
Rough & Rugged Lily companion

The Values & Virtues Book
... It's a God Thing!
Softcover 0-310-70257-7
Lily Speaks! companion

The Fun-Finder Book
... It's a God Thing!
Softcover 0-310-70258-5
Horse Crazy Lily companion

The Walk-the-Walk Book
... It's a God Thing!
Softcover 0-310-70259-3
Lily's Church Camp Adventure companion

Available now at your local bookstore!

Zonderkidz®